A BOUNCE BEFORE I DIE

SAM CHEEVER

ELECTRIC PROSE PUBLICATIONS

PRAISE FOR SAM CHEEVER

Villains, Annoying Assistants, and Monsters...Oh My!

My best friend had nothing to do with bouncing or monsters until something went terribly wrong in my new job. Suddenly she's missing, and the rumor is that a nest of monsters might have her. Those monsters are about to meet their match. I'm going to go medieval on their furry butts. If only I can figure out how to control my bouncing magic for five solid minutes.

I just hope Molly will forgive me for bringing her assistant Rog along on the rescue mission. The man has taken *annoying* to levels heretofore unknown. Believe me, I've tried to shake him. But he's like a giant octopus with a thousand tentacles. He insists he needs to go with me on the rescue. Unfortunately, the man has even less sense than he has magic. And he has zero magic.

Something tells me this is going to go badly.

STAY IN TOUCH

Sam doesn't give away a lot of books. But she values her readers and, to show it, she's gifting you a copy of a fun book just for signing up for her newsletter!

SIGN UP HERE!
https://samcheever.com/newsletter/

1

GIVE THE RAT SOME CHEESE

"Rog, I swear to the goddess I'm going to throttle you if you don't step back," I said.

Molly's assistant cocked a bony hip and fixed his expression into a look of disgust even the "get off my lawn guy" would envy. "We've had this discussion a thousand times," he said in a thoroughly disgruntled tone. "I'm right and you're wrong. There's nothing more to say. Now step aside grasshopper and let the sensei do his work."

I grabbed the nearest piece of wood and brandished it in his direction. "Step back Lackofsensei. You are physiologically and emotionally ill-equipped to assemble this desk."

Hands on hips, the pushy assistant glared at me, his brown eyes bulging with rage. Since both of us were around five feet seven inches tall, we met eye-to-eye across the battlefield, Molly's Spring designs surrounding us like fancy cloth soldiers. "Woman, you rarely make any sense. But that excrement is beyond ridiculous. Why would I be ill-equipped to tackle this simple project?"

I snorted to ward off a barrage of snarky responses. He'd really left himself open on that one. But I took the high road...or as high as it was possible for me to go at the moment. "Everybody knows that the male of the species doesn't read directions. Even though you're a beta male at best, you apparently inherited the instruction-resistant gene."

Rog launched himself at me, his bony frame hardly creating a backdraft as he chest-bumped me into the desk we'd been struggling to assemble. Unfortunately, instead of a sleek example of Swedish simplicity, it looked more like an alien pod. Parts stuck out from strange places. We'd run out of screws and bolts five minutes into the project. I was pretty sure that one of the drawers had been installed backward. And there was a strange slit in the desktop that I didn't think was supposed to be there. The thing might as well have been made for ET since I was pretty sure the assembly directions had been written by little green men.

Yeah, I know. I'd just accused Rob of not following the directions. But there's a difference between not reading and reading but not understanding a set of badly crafted instructions.

A tiny woman swept past us on a wave of flowery scent and glossy black hair. Molly rolled her eyes so hard I feared she'd crack her eye sockets. "Sweet Cherubs on a crescent moon!" she exclaimed on her way by. "You two are worse than my sister's teenagers. Just leave it. I'll put the thing together after I finish doing everything else you were supposed to do today."

Molly's diatribe shamed me and I frowned. Rounding on her annoying assistant, I focused such malevolence on him that my brain conjured a picture of a twitching pink nose with whiskers and big, rat teeth. It looked so real it startled me.

I needed to get hold of my temper before I started attacking the man with mis-assembled desk parts.

Sighing, I extended the board I'd been clutching in a gesture of goodwill. You'll have to forgive me if I cocked my arm into a throttling position with the offering. I'm only human after all. "If you can figure out where this goes, I'll take back my mean thoughts about men not reading directions."

Rog crossed his arms over his skinny chest and glared at me. "What about the mean thoughts you were having about me?"

I curled my lip. "Don't push your luck."

A soft sigh traveled in our direction from across the room, where Molly was pulling racks of designer duds around in an attempt to perfect the showroom's feng shui.

I opened my mouth to relent when the rat-face from seconds before reappeared, the tiny black eyes and nasty mouth slashing past inches away from my face on a shriek and a hiss.

"Ah!" I yelped, caught off guard. A beat later, I realized what was happening. "No, no, no, no, no!" I chanted, reaching frantically for the place of serene control that Justice had been trying to help me find.

Another rat joined the first, the two of them mere inches from my face when they leaped into the air. I ducked as the vision sifted away into nothing, fighting to concentrate on my control.

"What are you doing?" Rog asked in his usual nasally tone.

"Huh?" I asked stupidly. Shaking my head, I clenched all my muscles as if that would keep the bounce from coming. That, actually was the exact opposite of what Justice had been trying to teach me.

His deep, sexy voice slid across my thoughts. It was almost enough to distract me into calming the heck down. "*Close your eyes,*" his sonorous voice intoned in my mind. "*Take deep breaths. Think about easing into your bounce rather than being ripped into it.*"

Given that I'd been thrown into the traveler gig with zero warning and no preparation, Justice had been trying to get me up to speed for the last several weeks. We'd eschewed training in weapons and fighting since I'd been a cop for decades before I'd retired with the now defunct notion of relaxing more, reading lots of books, and sleeping as much as I wanted in between buying copious pairs of shoes.

Since I'd been coopted into my role as traveler—a sort of inter-dimensional cop—rather than recruited into it or joining by choice, I'd known nothing about the job when the previous traveler had popped out of thin air and magically transferred her job and responsibilities to me before promptly dying at my feet.

After learning to deal with my new future, I'd done my best to succeed. But I'd been shocked and slightly delighted to learn my new job actually came with magical skills. For example, I was supernaturally good with knives of all kinds. Apparently, I also had inner sight, which I had no idea how to use. But mostly, Justice and I had been practicing my bouncing skills, since that was the part of the job I needed and used the most. I was pretty bad at it. So bad, in fact, that I'd bounced over another traveler's gig in my first weeks as a traveler and nearly killed us both. For me, bouncing was basically a messy shift between dimensions and locations, meant to stop illegal inter-dimensional travel. For travelers who knew what they were doing, bouncing was much more elegant and targeted. I won't say I had no skill when it came to bouncing. But I definitely had no control.

Which was a massive problem.

Without warning, oversized rectangular teeth framed by stiff quivering whiskers snapped at my face, and I jumped as the vision slid through me and disappeared.

"You look like a toddler trying not to pee her pants," Rog snarked.

My eyes snapped open. "Pee," I said, then nodded. "Yeah, I need to pee." I pointed toward the restroom at the back of the store. But before I could turn away, Rog's face turned ratty again. I still had hopes that I could clamp down on the bounce until his mouth opened and he hissed.

I had a sense of water rolling over me and I knew I was a heartbeat away from bouncing.

Snatching the board away from Rog, I took off. I dove behind a rack of faux-farmer fashion just as the bounce grabbed hold and ripped me into the next world, one hand wrapped around a pair of white denim overalls with bling on the front that was shaped like a pocket.

I slammed into the ground, skidded three feet on my knees, and barely managed to throw myself backward to stop my forward motion before I crashed into a light pole. A distant chorus of hissing greeted me as I slowly climbed to my feet, listening to the sound of heavy footfalls heading my way.

I leaned over and put my hands on my grass-stained knees, groaning. White denim flopped in my hand and I glared down at the piece of clothing, noting the mud stains that hadn't been there when I'd grabbed it in a fit of desperation. I sighed, realizing I was going to have to pay Molly back for the damaged outfit.

The darkness leaped in my direction. Scary red eyes glowed eerily as an enormous, furry form went vertical and planted massive paws on my shoulders. I grimaced as a huge tongue slathered me from chin to hairline and gagged at the putrid stench the doggy kiss left behind. "Ugh!" I whined. "Dog breath." Elvo barked happily, bouncing around my feet in frantic canine bliss.

Another form stepped out of the darkness and my mind went blank as I slid a hungry gaze over a man who could only be described as tall, dangerous, and sexy. A former cop in my fifties, I'd spent a lot of my life looking for justice. But I'd never known finding him could be so inspiring. I wanted to rub myself all over him and purr a sexy suggestion into his ear, but I was still annoyed that my new job, a job I'd never asked for and mostly didn't want, was taking over my life. So, I narrowed my gaze on Justice instead. "I was in the middle of something important, you know."

His deep-set sapphire eyes seemed to spark in the moonlight, though that wasn't possible given the cloud-covered sky. "I take it you didn't manage to control your bounce again?"

Irrational anger, directed at him because I was feeling weak and inept and hated the feeling, brought heat into my cheeks. I didn't think I'd made a sound, but something about my present mood warned Elvo that he needed to be somewhere else. Whining softly, the big Hellhound mix turned on his furry heels and trotted to a spot behind Justice, dropping onto his belly in the thick grass.

My irritatingly sexy guide grinned. "Did you at least slow it down?"

Biting back a sarcastic response, I considered his question. After a beat, I had to admit that I had, if only for a few seconds. I sighed. "I saw rat things."

Justice's smile faded. "Rat shifters. Nasty things. One of the few monsters whose humanoid form is almost as repugnant as their animal shape." He glanced around as the moon came out from behind the clouds and I frowned up at the sky, realizing it didn't look right. "The moon is red."

He nodded. "Under the blood-red moon, monsters dance and croon, with flashing fangs and slashing claws, they rip the world to ruin."

I blinked. "Huh?"

"It's a childhood poem my ma used to recite. One I'd like to forget."

"No kidding." I couldn't help wondering what kind of childhood my guide had. "Where are we?"

That question wasn't as straightforward as it should have been. When I bounced, I was just as likely to change dimensions as geographic location.

"Aqua." He winced.

According to Justice, there were at least a dozen dimensions, which had been news to me since I'd always assumed I'd lived in the only one. However, I'd been assured we only worked with a few of the dimensions. There was Terro, otherwise known as Earth and its universe; Aere, a place of winds that could scour the skin off a body in minutes rather than hours; and the world of monsters, called Igne.

Then there was Aqua.

I frowned. "I thought you said we rarely got called to Aqua." It seemed the land of water didn't often need our help chasing dimensional boundary breakers.

"Rarely is not never," he said, wincing.

Apparently deciding I was over my snit, Elvo got up and trotted back to me, dropping to his belly on top of my feet. Not *near* my feet, but *on* them. Judging by the newly flattened aspect of my toes, I guessed he weighed around three hundred pounds. I tried to extricate my poor feet from the crushing weight and failed. Glancing around, I asked, "Where's the water?" My understanding was that, like its name, Aqua was a place of copious amounts of water. Yet we were standing on grass-covered ground.

Rather than respond verbally to my question, Justice hit a button on a large, lantern-type device I hadn't noticed until he'd turned it on. It flared to life, sending a bright white illumination around us. My guide held the lantern up and the light spread into the distance. The ground glistened in the moonlight, reflecting the bloody tint of the oversized orb high above us.

"Why does it look glossy?"

Justice hit another button and all the light tightened down into a single beam, which spread further into the distance. As the beam of light settled, a sleek white creature speared upward, twisting its muscular form in the air before bending to plunge downward again without a sound. The creature severed the ground with a knife-like precision, triggering a soft splashing sound as liquid rose up to mark the spot where it had disappeared.

Justice turned in a slow circle, illuminating the same glossy surface all around us.

I swallowed hard, realizing finally that we were standing on what appeared to be a fifty-foot-wide patch of land, in the middle of a literal sea of water.

Then, with a soft crackle of electricity, the light atop the light pole finally kicked on, and the space where we stood seemed to shrink beneath the overwhelming presence of water, reaching into the horizon all around us.

"Sweet cherubs on a crescent moon," I muttered as ice slid down my spine. "That's a lot of water."

2

YEAH, BUT CAN YOU SWIM?

"I feel like this question might be late in coming," Justice said, his gaze on the big canine cavorting goofily at the water's edge. "You do know how to swim, right?"

I gaped at him like something that belonged in all that water, lips flapping. "Are you serious? We have to get into the water?"

He glanced around. "There doesn't seem to be anything to capture or defeat here on the grass."

I let his words sink in for a beat, feeling them hit my brain like drops of burning lava. "I..." Swallowing hard, I tried desperately to gather my courage back up.

"Rae? You're scaring me."

I closed my eyes, thinking about my safe little apartment and seriously considering trying to bounce back that way. Of course I remained where I was, on a tiny piece of solid ground completely surrounded by water. No bridges. No boats. No options except to enter the black nightmare filled with millions of critters I was pretty sure were going to try to eat me.

In a vain attempt to soothe my nerves, I focused on Elvo slapping a huge paw on the surface of the gently undulating water. He jerked forward with every slap, biting at the resulting splash, his tail whipping happily behind him.

"Talk to me, Rae."

I forced my gaze to Justice. "I can swim..."

He visibly relaxed, his shoulders coming off square.

"Technically."

He went taut again. "What does that mean? Technically?"

I struggled to find a way to explain, but nothing I came up with left me with any dignity. I finally just went with the terrible truth. "I know how to swim, but I'm terrified of water. Especially large, deep bodies of water." When he just stared at me, I gave in to the need to clarify. "I was thrown off a fast-moving boat in the ocean once. I nearly drowned."

That was true as far as it went, but my explanation didn't even come close to the terror of being swamped by waves that rose five feet over my head or being bumped by a shark as I struggled to stay above water. "Let's just say the experience scarred me for life."

He seemed to pull himself out of whatever funk he'd fallen into and nodded. "Okay, well, I have bad news for you. We're going to have to go into that water."

I closed my eyes, fighting to breathe.

"Worse, you're going to have to bounce us there."

My eyes shot open. "What? Are you serious? What happened to all those warnings you keep giving me about bouncing multiple people? I thought I was too new at bouncing to do that?"

"Technically..." his lips quivered as he used my words against me. "...you *are* too new. But you've done it now, a few times, and your recovery rate has been better than average."

"Better than average!" I shrieked. "Have you forgotten that I'll be at the bottom of that ocean or whatever at the end of this bounce? How do you expect me to recover when I'll be worn out and terrified?"

"Technically…"

I think I might have growled a little.

He gave in to the smile. If the lantern beam hadn't been illuminating his face, I probably wouldn't have noticed the tightness around his eyes that told me he was worried. "…you're fully capable. What you're concerned about is purely in your head. You just need to not give into the fear."

"Ah!" I threw up my hands. "Silly me. Why didn't I think of that?"

He shrugged. "Beats me. You ready?"

Sarcasm was apparently lost on interdimensional guides.

My fingers tightened around the desk board I was still clutching. I took a step toward Justice and bumped into a big, warm, panting lump whose eyes were glowing extra red in the darkness. Elvo slathered the back of my hand with a really wet kiss.

"Ugh," I groused, wiping my hand on my jeans. But he'd managed to distract me enough that I lost my desire to pound Justice about the head and shoulders with my board. "Okay, tell me what we're trying to do." I had a thought that gave me a tiny bit of hope. "Wait. Where are the rat things? Rats don't live in the water. Maybe we're in the wrong place."

I knew immediately, from the look of pity on Justice's face, that I wasn't getting out of going into the water.

He shook his head. "Haven't you ever heard the phrase, 'rats deserting a sinking ship'?"

I cast a look out over the endless display of black water, frowning. "What ship?"

"It's out there. You just can't see it because it's dark."

"Then how am I supposed to find it?"

He shrugged, glancing at his wrist. Elvo dropped onto the grass with a groan and flopped over onto his side. They both appeared to be waiting. I had no idea for what. It didn't take me long to find out.

The world swayed sideways, darkened to charcoal, and erupted into a strange echo that sounded like something big shifting beneath the water.

"Breathe!" Justice yelled, the sound of his voice disconcerting as my vision and my presence on the tiny plot of land dissected and skewed away from each other.

Elvo barked in the distance, the sound not in the least frantic.

They're both crazy, I thought. And so was I for letting myself get...

One minute I was breathing air, and the next I was immersed in water. A cold, sodden weight pressed down on me, compressing me onto a surface that was harder than I'd expected.

Sand. My head whipped sideways and I spotted the shifting form of something hunkered on the dark sand.

As I realized where I was, I panicked, my arms flailing against the cold, black water and my mouth opening for a scream. A big hand slapped over my mouth as Justice's form appeared in front of me. His wavy light-brown hair swayed around his head and his features looked soft under the watery haze of our environment.

He motioned toward a dark, hulk of a structure above us, presumably riding the surface of the water, and grabbed my hand. I fought him, panic making me struggle unreasonably against his touch.

A big, furry lump bumped into me, nearly knocking me

to the ground. My gaze whipped toward Elvo, panic tripling as I saw the alarm in his blazing red eyes.

It was enough to pull me out of my fear. Digging my fingers into Elvo's thick fur, I stared at the nearby ship and pictured movement. The magic hesitated a beat. My chest felt as if it might explode if I didn't get air soon. But worse, the dog in my grip had gone very still and started to sink.

The world bent and hiccupped.

We slammed into a damp wooden surface that was thankfully not under water and I fell to my knees. "Elvo!" Dripping and vibrating with cold, I shoved at his chest with some vague hope of pushing the water from his lungs. "Justice, help him!"

"He's not dead, Rae. Hellhounds go into a kind of stasis when their systems are stressed. He'll be fine."

"He doesn't look fine," I said, my tone sharper than I would have liked.

"Let me see." The big man shouldered me aside and placed his hands over Elvo's broad, sodden chest. "Come on, son," Justice muttered. "Stop playing around and breathe."

Nothing was happening and I barely bit back a scream. Elvo was perfectly, terrifyingly still. His eyes were closed and his massive form wasn't moving.

"Justice?" I asked, tears burning my eyes. I fought the tears. In all my years as a cop, I'd never cried over a victim. I couldn't let myself weep, because if I did, all the carefully constructed strength and purpose would crumble away and leave me limp and soppy.

I lay my head on the big dog's chest, praying for the sound of a heartbeat. "Come on, Elvo," I whispered. "You can't leave me alone with this guy."

Justice grunted softly, and I noticed a soft, silvery glow was pulsing from his hands.

Still, nothing. No sound. No movement. No annoying licks. What I wouldn't give for an annoying lick at that moment. The stench of dog spit would be like a gift.

Thump.

I jolted, my hands wrapping around one thick, black leg. "That's it..."

Thump.

I risked a glance at Justice. His face was too pale and his eyes held a weariness I hadn't seen before. But still his hands fed magic light into the downed dog's chest.

Thump...thump...thump...

The leg in my grip moved slightly. I lifted my head. "Yes, that's it, come on, boy."

It shifted again, harder, and whacked Justice's arm.

Justice pulled away, straightened from the crouch he'd been in, and stumbled backward, hitting the stained wood of the ship's floor hard enough to damage something.

"Sweet cherubs on a crescent moon!" I yelled, jumping up and running over to make sure he wasn't dead.

Elvo struggled to get on his feet, whining softly. I wasn't sure if he was whining over Justice going down or because he was in pain himself. "Lay still," I yelled in his direction. "Rest," I said more softly.

Elvo whined one last time and stopped struggling.

"I can only handle one of you at a time," I told him, and Elvo gave a watery sigh, then succumbed to a coughing fit that presumably expelled some of the liquid from his lungs.

I bent over my guide, alarmed by his paper-white face. Grabbing his hand, I gasped at the icy feel of his flesh. "Justice?" I glanced around, trying to find something I could use to warm him.

A heavy thumping sound brought my head jerking up. I stared at the raw wood ceiling, realizing that whatever was up there was no more than the thickness of a half-rotted board away. We seemed to have landed in the hold of the ship, the curved sides slick with wet. As I watched, the wood of the hull seemed to curve inward against the pressure of the ocean beyond. It left behind a fresh trickle of water as it bulged back out, creaking loudly enough to make my pulse spike.

Seeing nothing to warm Justice with, I stretched out next to him and wrapped my limbs around him as best I could. With a speed that caused my eyes to narrow, his arms came around me and pressed me tight. He sighed, his eyes still closed.

His big body leeched warmth from me and I started to shiver, but that didn't last long, as the feel of his very masculine form against mine created its own kind of heat. I started to feel uncomfortable with our position and tried to pull away. "Um, Justice?"

His lips twitched and I would have extracted myself from his grip, but for the full body shudder that clacked his teeth together. The skin of his arms beneath my hands was still like ice. He wasn't getting warmer.

Another thud above our heads was followed by a terrible hissing sound and several shrieks. It sounded as if the rat things were battling it out on the level above us.

I experienced a sense of horror as I realized I would be fighting them alone. Me and my alien desk board. I had a moment of panic as I realized I was no longer holding the board. It wasn't much, but it had been my only weapon. Casting my eyes around the dimly lit space, I spotted it sticking out from under Elvo. Grimacing, I realized I'd never be able to yank it free from the heavy body.

A moment later I ran out of time anyway.

3

DESERTING A SINKING SHIP

A series of thuds reverberated above our heads. The hissing had grown in intensity and it was clearly coming closer. I kept my gaze on a large hole in the ceiling and below it, the pile of slivered wood that had probably been some kind of staircase. Extricating myself from Justice, I crawled quickly toward that pile. My first glance told me there were no pieces big enough to use as a weapon. But if I was right in my assessment, those things above our heads were really big rats. And it sounded as if there were a lot of them.

Right on cue, a deadly hiss sliced the air. I shuddered with revulsion as I looked up into the hole and saw a terrifying visage staring down at me. The thing looked exactly like a rat, except for its size, which resembled a large dog with pointy claws on "fingers" that seemed way too much like human hands. The deadly-looking claws were curved around the edge of the hole and covered in gore.

A dark shape slammed into the rat peering down at me. With a series of growling hisses, the two nasty creatures flew away from the hole to slam against something that reverberated through the half-rotted boards of the ship.

"I hate rats...I hate rats...I hate rats..." I chanted between violent shuddering as I dug through the broken staircase. Several large splinters later, the battling rats landed atop the hole above my head, slicing away a good part of the light I'd been using to see.

Trying to block the violence of the battle out of my mind, I pulled several inadequate but better than nothing sticks of wood from the pile.

The darker rat which, I realized with dismay, was half-again larger than the first rat, finally rose up on its back paws and bit down on the smaller rat's body, flinging it away with a triumphant squeal.

The resulting shudder as the loser landed set off a series of creaks that ended with more water oozing through the hull.

But that was the least of our problems.

Without warning, the victorious rat dropped through the hole in the ceiling, nearly smacking into me as it hit the slick wet floor and skidded.

I skittered backward with a terrified shriek. Later, if I lived through the current encounter, I'd spare myself a minute to feel embarrassed that I'd screamed like a girl. But I had no time to indulge in the luxury of mortification at the moment.

Its ugly, hairless tail swinging, the rat dropped to all fours and ran at me, its long feet slapping wetly on the floorboards.

I barely had time to react. Lifting my hands, I stabbed the sharpest of the two boards I'd grabbed toward the creature in the hopes of impaling it.

The board hit the thing's rhino-like skin and slipped

sideways, sinking into the crease between the rat's bent limb and its nearly hairless chest.

The creature squealed in pain, but its beady black eyes glowed yellow with a fiendish light. It snapped enormous, too-sharp teeth at me, barely missing the exposed skin of my forearm.

Pain sheared down my side and I realized the repulsive beast had managed to score a hit when I'd lifted my arm. It had teeth that were made for ripping meat and they'd done their job on me. With a sense of deep horror, I saw that my skin flapped over a wound that was gushing blood.

I felt faint the minute I saw the wound.

Stumbling backward, I clutched the remaining shard of wood in a shaking hand, my options narrowing.

The shadows shifted in my peripheral vision and Justice shot toward the rat, the alien desk board clutched in his big hands.

I pressed my tattered shirt over the wound on my side and sat back, praying my guide didn't need my help for a minute or two. A heartbeat later, Justice slammed against the wall beside me, a blood-painted rip dissecting the front of his shirt. He still clutched the board in one hand, but it was half the length it had been, the end splintered with rat-tooth markings.

Justice landed on his shoulder and hip, groaning as he pushed himself into a sitting position. "Any ideas?"

"I was thinking it might be time to bounce home."

Justice looked as if he was considering it, but then sighed, nodding toward the end of the ship where Elvo seemed to be taking a nice nap. "We can't. We have to close that portal or these things are going to be walking the streets of Terro."

I blinked. The idea of seeing the rat monsters running

around at home was too horrible to contemplate. Without warning the monstrous rat leaped past us and ran, clawed feet digging into the half-rotted wood. It was heading straight for the portal.

Ten feet, eight, six, five feet away...

Justice and I shoved to our feet. He took off running. I snagged the inadequate remains of my earlier weapon and took off after him.

Three feet, two feet, one...

Elvo's head shot up and his massive jaws wrapped around the rat's left foreleg, giving it a mighty yank.

The thing went down, clawing and snapping in a rabid attempt to win its freedom.

Elvo used the rat's weight to lever himself off the ground and, tail happily wagging, picked the nasty thing up and flung it away from the portal.

Squealing in fear, the rat sailed right at us. Justice leaped to one side and I...I...my mind went blank. I didn't even have time to scream before the nasty thing hit me in the mid-section and sent me flying right along with it. We slammed onto the floor, splashing salty water everywhere with the concussion of our landing, and hydroplaned all the way to the other end of the ship.

Luckily, the wood was softish because of the amount of water it had soaked up and it gave a little when my back hit rather than cracking my spine.

Unfortunately, my rodent friend went into immediate attack mode as we slid toward the ground, which earned me a long, bloody gash on one arm.

"Ouch!" I screamed, pounding on the thing with the too-small board.

I would have yelled at Elvo, but I was too busy trying to keep snapping rat teeth away from my throat.

The rat stiffened suddenly, its mouth gaping wide, and collapsed at my feet to expose a panting, wild-eyed Justice. The pitiful remains of my alien desk board was sticking out of its back.

I sighed. "I suppose that won't still work in Molly's desk?"

Justice snorted out a laugh.

"Woof!"

Our gazes slid toward the dog. I glared at the big goof. "Thanks for flinging a giant rat at me," I said.

"Woof!" Elvo's tail enthusiastically smacked the air behind him. He bounced happily, tongue lolling and whined as his gaze locked on the ceiling above our heads.

"Uh, oh," Justice said.

"Uh, oh?" I didn't like the sound of that. "What does that mean?"

Justice grimaced. "I picked a great time to be without my knives."

"Yeah," I said. "Where are your knives?"

"I dropped them out there in the water."

"Squeaaaaaalll!"

My gaze shot up to the hole in the ceiling, which was right over our heads.

Because of course it was.

"Why'd you do that?" I yelled as I tried to count the moving rat heads crammed into the hole. I was up to four when Justice responded indignantly. "If you'll recall, Traveler Kitt, I was a little busy drowning at the time."

I grudgingly admitted to myself that was a valid excuse. But it wasn't going to do anything to help us in the current situation. "So, how are we going to keep these things from getting through the portal?"

Elvo trotted over and looked up at the rat faces gathered

above us. He growled softly for a beat and then lunged upward, big teeth snapping at empty air as the whole group reared back out of the way.

I scratched the big dog behind his floppy ears. He squinted his eyes in pleasure and one back leg flailed vaguely toward his belly. I shook my head. He was such a needy baby. "How many of those things can Elvo take on at once?" I asked Justice.

The heads were back, hissing and snarling as more of them tried to cram into the space.

"Three or four, maybe."

I did a quick count. There were six heads sticking through the hole.

"That leaves one apiece for us." I grimaced. "I'd give anything to have a real weapon right now."

He nodded his agreement.

The big ship groaned around us, shuddering like a blood virgin in a room full of vampires. It gave me an idea. "How hard would it be to drown the rats?"

Justice slid a worried glance my way. "What exactly do you have in mind?"

"Nothing specific, I'm afraid. Only a vague idea."

He sighed. "They can swim. We'd have to trap them in the lower level while making sure they couldn't get to the portal or they'd escape."

A nearly impossible task.

"Maybe if we..." I never got a chance to finish that sentence. Another shuddering groan was all the warning we got that we were out of time. The hull bulged inward, giving a long, shuddering growl as if fighting against the indomitable force of the surrounding water pressing down on it. The water receded briefly, sucking the bowed wall out with it, and then slammed back into us. I was thrown off my feet and flung against the opposite wall, a roaring sound obliterating everything else as a ton of water rushed through the newly torn breach in the hull. The frothy water swirled around us in violent eddies that made it nearly impossible to keep my head above water, a dirty foam gathering along the edges of everything solid that didn't move.

I barely heard the nearby splash, but it immediately swamped me in debris-clogged water and I went under.

With my eyes tightly closed, I was unable to avoid the muscular, clawed limb that sliced bloody ribbons across my back. I bowed away from the claws, my eyes snapping open to introduce a new level of agony as salt water burned them like a flame.

Somehow I kept my eyes open and the burn eventually eased to a pain I could mostly ignore. Fighting the pressure of the incoming water, I swam toward the surface. Large furred bodies with razor-sharp claws also battled the pressure surrounding the rupture, too often colliding with my efforts to survive as they fought for the same thing. Overlaying the danger and chaos of my situation, a throbbing, deep pain made my chest feel like it would explode if I didn't get air soon.

A strong arm wrapped around my middle and yanked. I flew upward, bursting free from the roiling water with a painful gasp.

"We have to stop them!" Justice screamed to be heard above the rush and growl of the water. I nodded, but had no idea what to do. Then it hit me. It was a bad idea. But it was all I had. I turned to him and our eyes met. His eyes widened. His head began shaking even as I pulled away. "No, Rae!"

I fought my way out of his grip, only to immediately find myself swamped by frantic and therefore deadly rodents.

Two of them converged on me as I was caught up in an undercurrent of water that seemed to be dragging everyone to the portal at the end of the ship.

A third flailed wildly in an effort to make it to the portal before its ratty friends. I was immediately swamped beneath the third and found myself fighting to hold onto their fur as I was submerged.

There was no time to think.

No time to panic.

There was only one thing I could do.

So, I did it.

Picturing the tiny island in my mind, I felt the world shift as I spread myself like a starfish and touched as many furry bodies as I could reach.

Agony sliced through me as the water rushed away from us. It was all I could do to hold on as my watery grave fell away and we were dropped painfully onto the hard, grassy ground of the small island.

Moving on pure instinct, I rolled to avoid being flattened by the large, wet body slamming to the ground after me. I yelped in pain as teeth sank into my calf, knowing I had to be free of them when I bounced again or I'd bring them back with me.

I screamed as the teeth ground down on my leg, compressing hard enough to break bone. Nothing I did worked to free me from the rat's bite. In desperation, I grabbed a rock and hit it on the head.

It only made the monster madder.

Which gave me an idea.

I flung out an arm and slammed the rock down on the next rat's head. Still dazed and fighting to stand, the monster turned its beady gaze on the rat that had hold of me.

I rolled up into a fetal position, doing my best to disappear as the injured rat attacked with a hiss and a growl. Claws slashed the grass beneath me and whipped through the air inches from my body. Somehow I escaped the worst of the assault, suffering only a few shallow scratches.

The monster holding my leg released me to defend itself and I quickly scooted away. As soon as I was clear, I bounced back to the sinking ship, finding it nearly underwater. I emerged from the water, sputtering and gasping, and bumped into another rat.

I screeched and swung around, punching it in the chest. But it didn't react. Its glassy gaze stared sightlessly past me.

"Justice!" I screamed. "Elvo!"

No response.

I screamed for them again, shoving dead rat bodies away as I swam and searched. I stopped beneath the hole to the upper level and screamed their names, praying they'd made it out of the water. "Justice?!" The water swirled noisily around me and I knew it was swallowing my screams. But Elvo was a dog...a big dog...and he should be able to hear...

"Woof!"

The sound was faint, but my gaze shot in that direction, finding the big canine clinging to a floating barrel, his head nearly touching the ceiling.

I shoved off the dead rat and swam, my arms aching from the struggle against the violent eddies of the water. As I got closer, I realized there was a second barrel. Justice was draped over it and he wasn't moving. Worse, it looked like his face was in the water.

"Justice!?" Panic swamped me, the loss of focus pulling me underneath the swirling sea. I fought my way back, my limbs weakening with the effort. When I finally broke free of its grip, I realized I was further from the barrels rather than closer.

I wouldn't be able to do it myself. "Elvo, can you swim with him?"

I barely heard his whine above the roar of the sea. But, as I set off again, my weary arms and legs barely moved me forward and debris smacked painfully against me with every stroke.

Elvo slid into the water and went under.

I suppressed panic as I continued to swim. A few beats later Elvo's head came up and he grabbed something trailing into the water.

He began to swim and the barrel holding Justice came with him. They fairly flew at me, the current pulling them through the murky water. Realizing it was inevitable, I stopped trying to swim and focused on keeping my head above water. Seconds later, Elvo slammed into me and I grabbed hold of the barrel, trying to hold Justice's head above the churning water as we sailed toward the portal at the end.

I glanced at Elvo. "Hold on, buddy. This might get a little tricky."

4

THIS IS YOUR FAULT!

I'd expected to wash out into reality in a rush of debris-clogged water. I'd anticipated the portal experience to be harsh and jarring, a kaleidoscope of seizure-inducing lights and colors that left me dazed and twitching.

With those expectations, the reality was somewhat anti-climactic.

One second we were heading for the portal and the next, we were lying in a pile of battered bodies and broken barrel on a gravel lot behind a large brick building.

A car horn barked in the distance and, farther still away from us, sirens pierced the normal night sounds of a familiar part of town.

Shrill laughter jerked my head around to find a group of young women passing the mouth of an alley between the building where we'd landed and the next one. I held my breath as they passed, fearing they'd look over and find a half-drowned Hellhound mix, his dangerously gorgeous partner, two dog-sized rats, and me, looking guilty and disheveled.

I needn't have worried. They were too wrapped up in

themselves to even notice us. A minute later, they'd passed us by and were headed on down the street.

With a sinking feeling that made my heart pound too hard in my chest, I thought I knew where they were going.

"Woof!" Elvo said, just before I was showered with moisture as he gave a hearty shake. I grimaced, my hands coming up to shield my face from the spray.

"Hey!" I said in a harsh whisper. "Go over there and do that," I instructed, pointing toward the other end of the parking lot. "And no more barking. We're on the down-low."

He cocked his head and grinned, showing wickedly sharp teeth in a sweet face. Instead of doing as I'd asked, he lowered his head and shoved at one of the dead rats.

I winced. "Yeah, I know. We need to get rid of them."

He lifted an enormous paw and started clawing at the deceased rodent.

"Stop that!" I whisper-yelled. "It's dead. It's not going any..." My mouth snapped shut as an arm came out from beneath the beast and I realized what Elvo was doing. "Oh. Sweet cherubs on a crescent moon!" I hurried over to grab Justice's flailing hand, giving it a pull. I didn't succeed in moving him at all. "get on the other side of this rat and pull it off him," I barked out.

Elvo trotted around and grabbed one of the monster's legs in his teeth, yanking hard.

I pulled on Justice as the rat started to move away and managed to get him free of it. He lay face down for a moment, his body heaving as he gasped and groaned.

I crouched down beside him. "Are you okay?"

After a beat, he turned his head and glared up at me through one bloodshot sapphire eye.

"What?" I asked, sounding more defensive than I would have liked.

"Do I *look* okay?"

I didn't want to tell him that he looked more than fine. Even half-drowned and disheveled, he was gorgeous. It wouldn't be appropriate to tell him that. And he'd probably get a big...bigger...head from the compliment. "You actually look a little ragged," I said instead, grinning.

He rolled over onto his back and groaned again. "Well, that was fun. Are we dead? Because if this is heaven, I want a refund."

"We're not dead. We went through the portal." I looked around, frowning at the familiar shape of the night.

He pushed to a seated position and looked around with me. Elvo lumbered over and scoured Justice with wet kisses until the guide shoved him gently away. "Thanks, buddy," he said, his lips twitching. "I feel much better now."

Dropping to his massive, furry haunches, the big dog panted happily.

Justice's expression suddenly changed to something that looked like a mix of irritation and surprise. "Don't tell me you killed all the rats by yourself."

I suddenly found the building rising over us in the night to be very interesting.

"Rae?"

"I didn't kill them all. You guys killed some of them. I bounced a few..."

He grabbed my arm as I swayed, suddenly feeling dizzy. "How many?"

The world around me spun and I would have hit the ground if it weren't for Justice's grip on my arms. I opened my mouth to respond but found I couldn't form the words. They got lost in a haze of dizziness and fell away from my brain. I lifted my hand and showed him some fingers. I have no idea if I showed him the right number. At the moment, I had no idea how many rats I actually carried to that little island.

"Four!" he yelled.

"Shhhh," I managed, trying to put my hand over his mouth.

He grabbed my hand and yanked it down. "Rae, bouncing that many creatures of this size will kill you."

I shook my head, staring at the fingers as I tried to drop one of them. I was pretty sure it had only been three rats in that bounce.

He snorted out a laugh. "Cursing me out won't help, Traveler Kitt."

I frowned, then realized only one, very expressive finger was sticking up. Shaking my head, I closed my eyes. "I'll be fine," I said finally, the words kind of slurry. "I just need a nap."

He sighed. "Let's get you home…"

My eyes snapped open. "The rats."

He scooped me off the ground as if I weighed nothing. I smiled at the thought. I weighed something. LOTs of somethings. Even in my twenties I hadn't been a small woman. And with a few years of muscle and living under my much larger belt, I was anything but small.

"Elvo's got this."

He turned around and started across the lot. I lay my head on his shoulder and sighed. My eyes shot open again as flame burst into the night. Elvo lumbered up to us with his doggy grin firmly in place. Behind him, the rats were being incinerated in the biggest bonfire I'd ever seen.

"People will see the fire," I objected.

"It'll be gone by the time they get here," Justice told me. "Now, close your eyes and sleep."

It was oh so tempting to do just that. But I couldn't. Not yet. "No. Take me to The Muddle. I need to check on Molly."

"Molly? Why?"

I fought the siren song of sleep, barely managing to keep my eyes open. "Because she's like two feet from that portal."

He jerked to a stop, staring up at the metal and brick building in front of us with a frown. Even from the back, The Muddle was easy to identify, due to the enormous chrome and wood sign hanging from the brick wall. "Oh."

"Yeah." I licked my lips. "I need to..." What? I needed to warn her there might be dog-sized rats hanging around her building? Obviously, I couldn't do that without telling her about all of it. And I couldn't do that either. I sighed. "I just want to make sure she's okay. Then we need to find the rest of the rats. Because, you know some of them made it through that portal before we got there."

The fact that he didn't argue made me worry. "Okay. We'll check on her." He turned to Elvo. "Stay out here. See if you can pick up their trail."

With a happy woof! Elvo was off, lumbering across the lot with his nose inches from the ground.

I KNEW AS SOON as I reached for the front door that something was wrong. My pulse spiked and my temples tightened, the blood rushing through my ears as panic slammed through me. "Justice," I said, the word taut with fear. I shuddered, fighting the almost irresistible feeling that I should turn and run.

He reached past me and nudged me back with his big body, easing silently through the door and into the darkened store.

I glanced at the big clock on the wall, noting that it wasn't even ten pm yet. "The store shouldn't be closed," I said softly as I limped away from him, giving us a wider reaction area.

He didn't respond, his gaze skimming the darkness as if he could see. If it weren't for the array of security lights on poles in the front parking lot, I wouldn't be able to see anything. I slipped past a round clothing rack and jolted to a stop, gasping in surprise.

Justice stopped on the other side the rack. "What is it?"

I closed my eyes, pulling a calming breath into my lungs and slowly releasing it. "Just a mannequin." The dark-eyed beauty with too-shiny limbs was wearing Molly's latest, Night on the Town wear, which consisted of skin-tight white jeans and a furry, leopard-skin halter top with a pair of ruffled black ankle boots made of buttery soft leather. My hand reached out to touch the boots before I managed to stop myself. "Sorry," I whispered to Justice.

He disappeared from sight and, a beat later, I heard the soft scuff of his boots about fifteen feet away. I limped slowly toward the back, my destination Molly's office.

As I stepped around a brick partition that Mols had hired a well-known local street artist to paint with a fashion parade of her "city" designs on a range of her favorite models, I noted how dark the hallway that fed the offices and restrooms was. Even the security lights Molly had installed along the baseboards were dark.

Another soft scuff behind me announced Justice's arrival. "Something's wrong," I whispered in his direction. "There should be some light back here."

Justice didn't respond. I turned around to find only the darkness. No Justice.

Shrugging, I moved slowly down the hallway, my body

aching more with every step. I stopped in front of the restrooms and took a moment to push the doors open and stick my head inside. "Anybody here?" I whispered into the darkness.

Silence.

I moved on, peering into Rog's office and hesitating when I saw the overturned furniture and general disarray. "Rog?" My whispers were becoming harsher as my panic level increased. I stepped into the office, lamenting the empty state of my hands. I'd have given almost anything for even a small knife at that moment. Anything to fight off a monster.

As I had the thought, I realized that I'd already jumped to the assumption that Mols and Rog had encountered some of our monster friends from the portal. That would be bad. Really bad.

As my stomach twisted with fear, I shoved that thought away so I could continue to think and react. My eyes finally adjusting to the darkness, I quickly searched the messy room, finding nothing useful except a broken chair. I grabbed a chair leg so I wouldn't be completely helpless against whatever was in the building.

Stepping back into the hall, I moved quickly toward Molly's office. The door was closed and the smoky glass window had been shattered. I tripped over something heavy and stumbled forward. Pain flared through my right big toe. Hopping on one foot, I swore silently several times, rubbing the soggy MaryJane I was amazed I was still wearing after the whole ocean, ship, rats, and portal thing.

"I should be wearing steel-toed boots," I muttered. Instead of the cute, arcilla-colored leather shoe with gold buckles and a cork midsoles with a short heel. Which were probably salt-water stained and ruined. I was afraid to look.

Another soft scuff had me swinging around in reaction, the chair leg raised for a strike.

A beam of moonlight sifting through the window behind Molly's desk painted the man standing there in ghostly light, leeching some of the color from his skin and turning his eyes to liquid, fear-filled black pools. I went completely still, my arm still raised and moonlight seeming to gather in his bulging eyes.

"Rog?" I whispered, my skin prickling with fear and awareness as the blackness surrounding us bristled with evil intent.

He blinked slowly, his tongue coming out to sweep across full lips that looked gray. "She's gone," he said, his voice broken. He shuddered, a violent reaction that told me he was as traumatized as he'd looked. I grabbed my phone from Molly's desk where I'd left it, switching on the flashlight. The light skimmed over Rog's torn, bloodied shirt and wavered on a bandaged forearm. "Did you wrap your arm with your tie?" I asked him, needing a moment to dive into what had actually happened.

She's gone, he'd said.

I knew what that meant, but a part of my brain wanted to pretend he hadn't said it.

Rog looked down at the makeshift bandage. He ran a finger over the burgundy silk tie. "I never liked this one anyway."

It was a strange thing to say, and it made me laugh. The laugh strangled in my throat and I coughed, the sound coming out half sob. "Who took her," I asked the stricken man standing a mere eight feet away.

If it was possible, his gaze filled with even more terror. His mouth opened and then slammed closed, pressing into a firm line. He straightened his narrow shoulders. Lifted his chin. And gave me one of his trademark glares. "I know this has something to do with your new job."

I started to deny it, but saw the fierce rage in his expression and let the accusation fall away unanswered.

He lifted his unbandaged arm and pointed a shaky finger at me. "This is your fault, Rae. Yours!" he said more forcefully. "You are going to fix it. And I'm going to help."

5

I CAN'T BEAR IT

I sat at Molly's desk, watching Justice clean and bandage Rog's wound with the first-aid kit I'd insisted Molly buy for the store. Running my hands through my short cap of curly auburn hair. I felt disheveled and filthy. I kept getting a whiff of a fishy smell I knew wasn't my imagination. I'd kill for a shower.

Though Justice had bandaged my assorted wounds and wrapped my leg, he hadn't had any of the magical ointment so they still hurt like the dickens.

Justice glanced my way and his brows peaked.

I stared back, knowing my eyes were probably too wide, the green of my irises overtaking the pupils as my eyes adjusted to the harsh change in light. I looked away from him, not wanting him to see how upset I was. Stretching out my legs, I carefully crossed them at the ankles and noted they looked slimmer than before, yet shaped with lean muscle. Becoming a traveler had been good for my physique. At five feet seven, I had long legs and a strong form, but not bulky. The decades of being a cop had kept me in shape until middle age had hit. Then age had touched my fine features with wrinkles, thickening my waist, and thinning the thick cap of auburn hair a bit. I didn't like the changes, but they weren't that bad, and I'd earned every single wrinkle I wore on my oval face.

"Where is she?" Rog suddenly demanded, yanking me from my thoughts.

"Huh?" I gave myself an internalized face slap. I sounded like a simpleton. "Molly?"

"Who else," he growled, tugging on his torn and stained shirt. "Where'd they take her?"

"Tell us what happened," Justice said, his voice kind. He began tucking items back into the first aid kit, giving Rog a moment to consider his question.

I wasn't so considerate. I was watching him like a hawk when the look of pure terror filled his eyes. Rog caught me noticing and frowned, skimming his gaze toward the door. "I don't know who it was," he said evasively. "I was in the back room, shaking out and racking the newest delivery of clothes." He plucked at his shirt with fingers that I noted were shaking. "I heard her scream and it threw me for a loop." His voice caught and he cleared his throat. "I. Hesitated." The way he said the words was like self-flagellation. Rog shook his head. "If I'd hurried..."

"You can't beat yourself up..." I started to say.

His head shot up, his expression enraged. "Who *should* I beat up then, Rae? You? Isn't this your fault? She never dreamed the weird stuff you've gotten yourself into would come back to bite *her*. Why should she? Who would ever expect..." His lips flattened, his eyes darkening with emotion. "*Who would expect that*?" he whispered.

"What did you see?" Justice asked.

Rog shook his head, suddenly surging to his feet. His small brown hands fluttered away from him as if he had no control. His gaze darted from side to side. "We have to help her."

Justice slid me a look. Our gazes met and I nodded just enough to let him know we were on the same page. Rog had clearly seen something from another dimension. Something terrifying. And judging by his appearance, something dangerous.

I nodded toward his shirt. "What tore your shirt?" I'd all but given up on the possibility that he'd answer us. I knew why. If he said the words aloud, it would make the monsters real. And if it became real, Rog would have to admit to himself that Molly was in real danger.

I knew from personal experience that wasn't a fun place to be.

He shook his head again and I thought he was refusing to answer. But he said, "It picked me up like I weighed nothing. It had terrible claws and smelled…" Frowning as if trying to come up with the right word, he finally said. "Feral."

"A dog?" Justice asked, testing the waters. The guide was smart. If Rog was still unable to admit what he'd experienced, he'd jump on the suggestion. "A big one, like Elvo?"

Rog hesitated, his chin lifting a tiny bit as if he intended to nod. But he didn't nod. He shuddered instead. The action so violent he nearly fell over. He had to grab onto the front edge of Molly's desk to keep himself upright. That was the moment I wondered if he had something else going on physically. Some kind of poison coursing through his veins or something.

"No," he said with unexpected conviction. "Not a dog. More like a bear." He nodded once as if that explanation pleased him. Yes, it would be strange for a bear to have entered The Muddle. But not as strange as a creature from a monster dimension.

"A bear?" Justice asked, his tone assessing.

"Yes. A bear." The tilt of Rog's chin all but dared us to argue.

We didn't argue.

Justice inclined his head. "Elvo's scenting the perimeter," he told Rog. "If there was a bear out there, he'll find the trail."

Rog nodded, crossing his skinny arms over his skinny chest. "When you track it, I'm going with you."

I was already shaking my head no.

Justice lifted a hand away from his hip, low enough that Rog wouldn't notice. I bit back the rejection of his idea I was about to voice. "Have you fought a bear before?" Justice asked.

Rog stared at him for a beat, clearly perplexed by the question. Finally, he shook his head. "No. But..."

"I've hunted bear," Justice told him. "I know their habits, strengths, weaknesses. If you come along, I'll have to worry about you instead of focusing on Molly. That isn't what you want, is it?"

His shoulders fell. "No."

Justice clapped a hand on Rog's bony shoulder. The smaller man tottered as if he might fall. The fingers on his shoulder curved to hold him upright. "I'll bring Molly back," Justice said.

Tears burned my eyes as I realized he shouldn't make that promise. Justice sounded sure. But nothing was definite in the world of monsters. Nothing was predictable. Still, I couldn't reprimand him. I needed that reassurance every bit as much as Rog did.

Justice looked at me. "You get him home. Elvo and I will handle this."

I surged upright. "No. I'm going with you."

"She's right," Rog said, earning brownie points from me. "She can help find Mols. Don't leave her here with me. Don't make me the cause of Molly maybe being lost because you didn't have the help you needed."

His plea was desperate but reasonable enough to make Justice hesitate. He glanced my way and I nodded. "I'm coming."

"It's not safe for Rog to be out there alone."

"That's okay," Molly's stubborn assistant said. "Because I won't be alone. I'm coming with you."

No amount of arguing changed Rog's mind. Finally, realizing we were losing precious time, I gave in, forcing Justice to follow suit. "You stay close and do exactly what we say when we say it, understood?" I told Rog.

The man's lips flattened and fire lit his gaze, but he nodded. "Understood."

He was totally going to do whatever he wanted.

Sighing, I moved to the locked metal cabinet at the back of the room. I picked up the candy bowl on the top and reached inside, finding the fake wood bottom and prying it up with my fingernail.

"This is no time for a snack," Rog said, his tone snotty and impatient. In other words, normal.

Ignoring him, I extracted the key hidden beneath the wood and unlocked the cabinet, pocketing the key. Since Rob knew about my hiding spot, I'd have to find a different one after we got Molly back.

The thought comforted me. We *would* get her back.

Opening the top drawer, I tugged a pile of clean clothing

aside and grabbed my gun and two knives. I handed Justice the knives and grabbed an extra magazine for the Glock.

When I turned around, Rog was staring at me gape-mouthed. He looked kind of gray.

"You had weapons!"

I thought he was horrified by their very existence in his sphere, but his next words changed my understanding.

"Why didn't you tell me those were there? I could have saved Molly."

Aside from the idea of Rog with a gun in his hand, which was enough to liquify my bowels, I was shocked he'd even consider using the gun. He was a self-declared peacenik and liked to call me a barbarian for believing in the equalizing quality of a good gun or blade. "I...ah..."

Justice nodded toward the door, saving me from having to respond. "I'll go first, you stay close to my heels," he told Rog. "Rae will take up the rear. Under no circumstances will you abandon that position."

Rog nodded without the attitude he'd given me.

Annoying.

We exited the store and walked out into a warm, dark night. I looked up at the security lights and gasped. Even in the darkness, I could see the bent and twisted lamps atop the poles. "Justice," I said softly.

His gaze followed mine and he stilled. No normal bear had done that. He didn't respond, but he glanced at Rog. "Stay close," he whispered.

Rog seemed to pick up on our worry. He was strangely quiet, a state I didn't think I'd ever seen him in, and did as he was told without argument.

The only voice I heard was Justice's as he swore at Rog to stop stepping on his heels.

The night air felt heavy and moist, as if rain were

trapped there, unable to fall. The sky was a mix of lead and charcoal, so dark I could barely see Justice fifteen feet away.

In front of me, Rog suddenly dodged sideways and my hand tightened on my gun, still jammed in the small of my back. Without warning, a tall form appeared in front of me and I sucked in a surprised gasp, the gun found my hand before I identified my foe. Then I laughed, realizing I'd just drawn on a sapling.

"What did that tree ever do to you?" a snide voice said from beside me.

Only decades of experience on the streets as a cop kept me from plugging Rog between his bulgy eyes.

My pulse pounding in my ears and my skin tingling with awareness, I eased a breath out between my lips and forced myself to relax. "You're going to get shot. You're supposed to stay close to Justice. Where is he?"

The whites of Rog's eyes were visible through the dark. They looked enormous. "I lost him. I figured he was with you."

6

WE'RE NOT IN KANSAS ANYMORE

"What do you mean you thought he was with me? You were right on his heels. Literally."

Rog's small form shifted in what I thought was a shrug. "He told me to stay and walked into that clump of bushes over there. When he didn't come back, I thought he'd circled around and was with you."

Something thumped against my ribs and it took me a minute to realize it was my heart. Justice was gone? He'd probably just gone ahead to scout out a safe route. Surely he'd be back. I opened my mouth to tell Rog to stay put but slammed it shut again. I was the annoying little twerp's only protection. Instead, I grabbed his arm, yanking him up against my side. I gave up trying to play it cool and clutched my gun. "No matter what happens, we stick together. You understand?"

The whites of Rog's eyes all but glowed in the darkness. His eyes looked huge. The poor guy was a nervous wreck. "Yeah?"

I frowned. "Are you asking me? Or agreeing to my demands?"

"Agreeing?"

My frown deepened. "What are you, a Valley Girl? You're ending every sentence with a question sound."

"I'm not?"

I growled. Which reminded me. My head came up and I peered through the increasingly hazy night. "Where's Elvo?"

"Maybe Justice is with him?"

"Okay, stop that!" I snipped, jerking him forward. Despite my concern for our predicament, I didn't miss Rog's sly smile as I started walking. He'd been tweaking me.

Jerk.

"Where are we going?" Rog asked me a few minutes later. I'd been marching forward with my head on a swivel, not thinking about a destination so much as trying to find Justice and Elvo. That was the moment I realized how dependent I'd become on the two of them. My partners. The thought would have made me smile if I wasn't so worried. "Don't ask questions," I told Rog.

He ignored me. Of course. "We're wasting time. We need to find Mols." His voice shook slightly. I glanced his way. "I am trying to find her."

"So, we're just going to wander around until what...we bump into her?"

"Maybe?"

He snorted, scraping a hand over his tear-drenched face when he thought I wasn't looking. The street had grown increasingly hazy, the fine mist that had drenched the air turning to a fog that swirled around our feet and seemed to be thickening with every step we took. Our footfalls made no sound at all, and our voices were muffled by the mist.

I jolted to a stop as I realized there was no traffic on the street.

"What is it? Did you hear something?" Rog asked.

There hadn't been any cars on the road for at least twenty minutes. While it wasn't all that unusual for the area around Molly's store to have light traffic, I'd never known it to be completely devoid of cars. I looked around, trying to discern our location through the fog, but realized with a start that I didn't recognize anything around us.

Rog seemed to realize the same thing. "Where are we?"

I didn't want to tell him I had no idea. We must have taken a wrong turn in the fog and ended up... Where? I knew Fort Wallace like the back of my hand, and I'd never seen the strange round-topped buildings with bars over the doors and windows. A nasty, fishy smell wafted past and ice found my spine.

"Ugh. What's that smell?" Rog asked, covering his nose and grimacing.

In the distance water lapped against a shoreline that shouldn't be there.

I whipped around, grabbing his arm. "You don't recognize this place?"

Rog yanked free of my grip. "Ow, Rae. Chillax."

"Tell me!" My strident tone seemed to reverberate around us, not breaching the mist but cocooning us in sound.

He glared at me. As I realized the night was no longer pitch black, and that I could see his expression. My gaze slid skyward. I swallowed hard. *Seriously?* My alarm must have shown in my face because Rog started to look up too. I yanked him forward again, not wanting him to see. "We need to keep moving."

I'd been hoping to distract him from the fact that there were three silvery planetary bodies hanging in the sky. Three. That could only mean...

"Is the thing that took Molly here?" Rog asked, his wide,

alarmed gaze skimming the night. "Is that why you're freaking out?"

"I'm not freaking out," I said in a harsh whisper, but I stepped up the pace as the foggy night changed form. The mist shifted around us, creeping and oozing evil as my pulse spiked into stroke range.

The fog had taken on a life of its own. It darkened and swayed, thinned and hissed, until it was all I could do to keep from shooting blindly into it. At one point I'd pulled the gun I was carrying and was pointing it blindly into the haze. The skin between my shoulder blades prickled with awareness and my hearing became hypersensitive. The problem was, I wasn't sure if what I was seeing and hearing came from inside my mind, or danced around us in the fog.

It wasn't until my brain registered Rog's harsh breathing that I realized we'd been running. I had a death grip on his wrist and I'd been pulling him with me. Rog wasn't built for that kind of extended workout. His face glistened with sweat and his skinny chest rose and fell as he struggled to pull air into his lungs.

I dropped his arm like I'd been scalded and stepped away. "I'm sorry," I told him, realizing finally that he'd been shouting at me.

He bent over, putting his hands on his knees and wheezing. "If...I...could...breathe...I'd really...yell," he assured me in between wheezes.

"I'm really sorry," I said. "I thought I heard something." Even as I made the excuse, I knew it was crazy pants. I scrubbed my hands over my face, finding it damp from the mist. My pulse still thrumming with alarm, I started to pace. "I thought..."

Rog finally straightened. He was still panting, but didn't

look as if he was in danger of dropping dead. "You're not even breathing hard, Rae. What's going on with you?"

Magic, I thought. Magic was what was going on with me. Ever since I'd taken on the traveler magic from a woman I'd never met before, I'd been changing. But I couldn't tell him that. "We should really keep moving," I said instead.

To his credit, Rog didn't groan or complain. He simply nodded and straightened. We started walking through the fog again. I worked to keep my strides steady but not too fast. Rog stayed quiet for a few minutes, but I could feel his thoughts as if they were part of the fog. "What?" I finally said, irritation painting my tone.

"We're lost, aren't we?"

My gaze skimmed the edge of the fog and the rounded outline of the buildings bordering the sea. I determinedly kept from looking up to see if there were still three moons in the sky. "You have no idea," I told him.

Silence floated between us for a few beats. Then... "We're not in Kansas anymore, are we?" Rog asked.

I barked out a laugh that turned slightly hysterical. It was only when I saw the suspicious shine in his eyes that I was able to bite off the hysteria and regain a sliver of composure. Aloud, I said, "No. We're not in Kansas anymore."

He nodded. "Will there be flying monkeys?"

His voice sounded small, and I wanted to kick myself for admitting what he already knew. Denial wasn't just a river in Egypt. It was also a comfort when life turned dark and scary. I shrugged. Unfortunately, in my new reality, flying monkeys were a distinct possibility.

The fog hissed and I jumped, my hand coming up with my gun as the shadows twisted and flew at me, all claws and fangs and rage. I'd fired off three shots before I realized the creature was down, its mouth open as it tried to breathe past the teeth clamping its throat closed.

I sagged downward in relief and horror. "I could have shot you!" I yelled at Elvo.

The big dog rolled his eyes in my direction and then jerked his head, breaking the giant rat's neck with an audible crunch.

Rog hopped from foot to foot, his hands twisting frantically in front of him. "That's..." He moaned softly. "Oh, my go..." He retched. "I'm gonna be..." He turned away and threw up, his body jerking violently with every expulsion.

A sympathetic retcher, I gagged and almost followed suit.

Elvo dropped his prize and trotted over, bumping me with his big nose to distract me. My hand found his silky mass of fur and clenched it as if it was the only thing keeping me on my feet. I dropped to my knees and buried my face in his fur. "I'm so glad to see you," I mumbled.

Elvo whined, bumping me again with his cold, wet nose. I sat back on my heels. "What? Have you seen Justice?"

The big dog turned away from me, his hairy tail whipping the air. When we didn't immediately follow, he barked. It was a deep, husky sound that reverberated around us and urged me forward.

"Show me," I said, somehow knowing that was what he wanted.

Elvo disappeared into the fog.

I straightened and grabbed the back of Rog's shirt. "Come on. Elvo will take us to Justice."

Rog retched again.

I gagged violently.

Elvo barked from somewhere out of sight.

"Stop that," I told Rog. "You're going to make me hork.

We can't just stay here puking all night. There might be more of those rat things."

That got him on his feet. Rog stumbled after me as I gave the dead rat lots of space and followed in Elvo's pawprints. "Those things aren't real," he informed me.

"Okay," I said, in no mood to argue.

"I mean it, Rae!"

I nodded. "Uh huh."

He sighed, but apparently my not arguing satisfied him for the moment.

For just a little while longer, denial would be our best friend.

7

DO TURTLES GROWL?

The building was really little more than a shack. It sat on what looked like a wooden dock, which stuck out into a frothy body of water whose parameters were indecipherable in the darkness.

The stench of dead fish was life-altering. I lived in fear that Rog would start gagging again and set me off. With that thought uppermost in my mind, I sent him a warning glare every few minutes. Molly's annoying assistant had gotten offended the first few times, but when I didn't clarify, he'd given up, only rolling his eyes at me.

Elvo stopped to examine something draped across the dock and then stepped over it, his big form shaking the dock as he trotted toward the shack at the end.

A horrible stench oozed up from the flattened, gutted creature stretched out over the wooden slats and, as we approached, a small army of tiny crablike creatures skittered away from the corpse, plopping softly into the water.

Ugh!

I forced myself not to look too closely at what appeared

to have once been some kind of snake-like fish, and stepped over it.

Behind me, Rog said, "Bleurgh!"

I retched in expectation. "Don't you dare!" I whisper-yelled over my shoulder.

"This is nasty," he replied.

"Shh!" I hissed. "Sound carries over water."

He snorted. "I doubt any of those rat things—which don't exist by the way—are going to swim up and snatch us."

Ahead of me, Elvo dissolved into the darkness, disappearing from sight. I stepped up my pace. "Do you really think the rats are all we need to worry about?"

When he didn't respond, I turned around and caught him staring out to sea. I followed his line of sight where the three moons painted the distant water in silver strokes. Something moved beneath the water. A thick, dragon-like form emerged and rolled across the surface, creating a series of humps that gave way, eventually, to a wide, fanlike tail that softly slapped the water as the creature dove out of sight.

"That thing was fifty feet long if it was an inch," Rog breathed.

My heart twisted at the look of pure terror on his face. But I knew I couldn't baby him, or he'd never survive what was ahead. "Hurry up," I hissed. "Justice and Molly might be in danger and you're just standing around gaping at fish."

He started walking again, his shoulders hunched. "That was no fish," he murmured crankily.

Good, I thought. Cranky was good. Cranky would distract him from wetting himself with terror.

I waited for Rog at the edge of the shadows, my skin prickling with tiny electrical shocks as the darkness shrouding the rickety structure beckoned me.

Magic.

I didn't want to know what was controlling the illusion. But I had a feeling I was going to find out. As Rog caught up to me, he gave a violent shudder and looked around. "What is that?"

I was honestly surprised he could feel it. "Nothing. Come on. We need to catch up with Elvo."

The truth was that whatever we were searching for was probably inside the shack. As I eyed the ramshackle, weather-worn structure, I came up with a dozen reasons off the top of my head why we shouldn't go in there.

But go in there we would. Because I had a strong suspicion the shack held the secret to both Molly's and Justice's disappearances.

Rog grabbed my arm as I started forward. "Rae?"

The determination in his voice had me turning back. I raised a brow in question, trying to ignore the sting of wild magic biting my skin.

"I'm not as weak and afraid as you think I am."

I wasn't sure how to respond to that. "Okay." That response felt wrong. But it was the best I could do. My mind was on other, more deadly things.

"If Molly's in danger, you can count on me to help."

His sincerity finally cut through my distracted thoughts. I smiled and patted his arm. "Good. Because I have a feeling I'm going to need all the help you can give me."

He nodded and stepped past me, into the darkness. I moved quickly to catch up, and ran right into him. He'd stopped dead in his tracks, his narrow body vibrating with fear.

I bit back a gasp, my hand finding his and squeezing it. Hard.

I stared at the creature standing ten feet away, my

breathing constricted as a wave of pure terror slipped over me.

Rog laughed. Actually laughed. "Seriously?" he asked, grinning my way, "You're afraid of turtles?"

I gave him a disbelieving look. "That's no turtle. It's literally the size of one of those small cars from that ocean movie." Okay. Maybe not literally. But close enough.

Rog frowned. "Water cars?"

"Of course not. Besides...focus."

"Why would there be cars in an ocean movie?" Rog argued.

Moving slowly, I reached out and grabbed his arm, trying to tug him behind me. He shook me off. "Rae, that's a tortoise. They're like the fluffy bunnies of the sea."

"If fluffy bunnies have sharp beaks and can smash you into a puddle by sitting on you." Not to mention the jagged edge of its massive shell and the dangerous-looking horn in the center of its head.

"I promise, that creature's not going to hurt anybody."

"How do you know? Are you some kind of expert on turtles?"

"I did have turtles when I was growing up. But no, I don't know all that much about tortoises."

"Then let's just give this one a wide berth. Remember, we're not in Kansas anymore."

As if to prove my point, the monstrous turtle lifted its head and growled, the sound bringing gooseflesh up all along my arms.

"Did that thing just growl?" I asked in a harsh whisper. As far as I knew, turtles didn't growl.

With a speed the big, clunky thing shouldn't have been able to muster, it lashed out at something in the water, coming up with a wriggling creature that had a nearly transparent round head and too many limbs. About eighteen inches across and probably around thirty pounds, the slimy-looking creature reminded me of an octopus, except that each tentacle had a crab-type claw on the end and the things appeared to be very stretchy. Without warning, one of them lashed out at Rog. He jumped back with a yelp and the claw barely missed. Another inch and he'd have been filleted by a fish.

Irony at its best.

The tortoise stretched its long, wrinkly neck, and the slimy, clawed critter slipped down its throat in a rapidly descending bulge, like a snake swallowing its prey.

"Ugh!" I said, grimacing.

"Was that an octopus?" Rog asked, his eyes even wider than usual.

I opened my mouth, realized I didn't know what to say, and closed it again. "Come on, we need to get to that door."

I nodded toward a wooden door in the wall nearest the tortoise. The door stood open but there was no sound coming from inside the building. That worried me.

"I don't think I want to get that close to the tortoise," Rog said.

"What happened to the fluffy bunny theory?" I teased.

He shrugged. "You were r...r...right. We're not in Kansas anymore."

I cupped an ear with my hand. "What did you say? I didn't quite hear you say that I was right."

"Don't push your luck, cop."

Despite my teasing, I was with him. Keeping distance between us and the oversized turtle was key to our survival. We stood staring at the door for a long moment. Finally, I said, "Let me see if there's another way inside."

He nodded and took two large steps away from the alien tortoise, crossing his arms over his chest. "I'll wait here."

I rolled my eyes. The shack took up half the width of the wide dock and the turtle was hogging most of what was left. We had a narrow band of about ten inches to work with. I spotted a small window about halfway down the weather-worn gray wood wall. "I've got something," I called out to Rog.

A beat later, his head popped around the corner, his normally carefully combed black hair sticking up in spurts all over his head. "What did you find?"

I pointed to the window.

He eyed the narrow ribbon of dock beneath my feet. "Um..."

I held up a finger. "Let me see if it's even big enough before we start planning logistics."

Rog put hands on hips and gave me a look. Like a chicken with attitude, he swayed from stem to stern, both brows lifted in perfect black arcs. "After seeing that slimy clawed thing, if you think I'm gettin' that close to the water, you're suckin' whiskey through a straw."

Since I rarely drank anything containing alcohol, I doubted that. "Whatever happened to I could count on you to help because you weren't a fraidy cat?"

His brows flattened out and dropped toward his eyes. "I said I'm brave, not stupid."

I bit back a snarky response. He really needed to stop giving me so much ammunition to work with. After all, I wasn't a saint. "Just stand there and wait. I'm going to see if I can get through the window." Since I probably outweighed him by thirty pounds and had bigger...erm...shoulders, if I could get through, so could he.

Putting my back to the wall, I scooted along the rough

surface. My shirt caught on the rough wood and tore as I wrenched myself forward. I barely even paid any attention to the rips. Between being dunked into salt water, rolling around in that filthy ship, and battling giant rats, my clothes were already destined for the trash.

And I didn't even want to think about how badly I smelled.

Distracted by unimportant things, I took a misstep and my foot slipped off the side of the dock. I yelped as I started to fall into the frothy water and threw up my arms. Somehow I caught hold of a bait pole hanging out over the sea and my fingers closed around it. I hung there, kicking my legs in an effort to regain the dock. Stars burst before my eyes as adrenaline kicked in. My heart was pounding hard enough to explode.

Below my feet...and not very far below them...dark shapes sliced through the murky water, their undulating forms taking on a sinister feel due to the lack of detail.

Something broke the surface beyond the end of the dock. Waves rolled off the enormous creature and slapped violently against the dock supports. I forgot all about those things swimming around below me, my eyes all but popping out of my face as a long, leonine head lifted above the surface. Oversized eyes the color of the ocean seemed to shine through the night as if the creature was lit with a glow from within. The monster's half-circle nostrils flared delicately as it scented me, and long curved teeth stuck out of its mouth like a series of ivory fish hooks.

Behind the head, a spiked hump rose from the water, stretching a good ten feet behind it. The body was slender and muscular, flexing and tensing as the waves broke over its scales. My brain went numb at the sight and I hung there, afraid to move.

Maybe it hadn't seen me yet. If I moved really slowly...

"What's taking so long, Rae?" Rog yelled, his head popping around the corner again.

Another spiked hump rose out of the sea and the monster that was floating easily on the surface cast its hungry gaze toward Rog.

"Ah!" Rog screamed, his obvious terror making him even more attractive as a potential snack. It was like putting butter and sour cream on a hot baked potato. Irresistible.

And with that, the creature shot in his direction.

I screamed as the enormous body slammed into me and my grip on the pole melted away. I dropped like a rock, bouncing off the meaty form of the monster and falling into the warm, black water. I slid downward, the liquid feeling more like syrup than water.

Something long and black bumped against me, and electricity zinged through my system, sending me into helpless spasms that removed the ability to control my own body. When the spasms eased, I realized I'd sunk deeper into the black water. I tried to swim, but my body was too numb to function. I was running out of time. My chest burned from lack of air. In desperation, I stretched out a foot, looking for the bottom, and instead felt a smooth rubbery surface beneath my shoe that wasn't stationary. It was better than nothing. I pushed off the big fish and hurtled toward the surface.

Above me, the water churned and throbbed with the sea monster's massive body. Distant screaming made me kick harder, spearing directly toward the enormous spiky creature attacking Rog.

Out of nowhere, something slammed into me and I flew sideways, slamming against the dock support nearest me.

The impact stunned me and my mouth opened, warm, thick water oozing over my tongue.

The dock shook as the monster's flailing tail smacked it again. The concussion yanked me out of my daze. I barely had time to consider what I was doing as I grabbed hold of the creature's fanlike tail and wrapped myself around it. Water rushed over me, the force making it nearly impossible to hold onto the slippery creature. I broke the surface of the water and caught sight of Rog. The creature had him in its mouth and he was pounding its snout, his body torn and bleeding.

I didn't have time to plan. I only had time to act. And I'd only get one chance to save him. As the fan tail reached the apex of its swing, before it started to descend back to the water, I let go and flew through the air. My trajectory was off. I'd hoped to land on top of the creature so I could distract it enough that it'd drop Rog. I was going to miss it by a couple of feet.

Plan B it was, then.

I'd really hoped to avoid Plan B. "Rog!" I screamed.

He didn't look my way. His head drooped to his chest and he was no longer shrieking. "Rog! Hand!"

His movements were too slow. He was starting to go limp. I feared I was already too late. But at the last moment his gaze lifted to mine, filled with hope, and he raised a limp arm. A second later our fingers touched. I grabbed onto him with everything I had.

And thought about my living room.

The world went hazy, shifted sideways, and then I hit something soft that screeched across the wooden floor as my weight slammed into it.

The second after I landed, another weight hit the couch beside me. That was the final straw. My elderly couch groaned long and low, and then split down the center and crashed to the ground in two pieces.

"Uhhhhhh," Rog groaned.

I shoved myself off my half of the broken couch and looked at him. "How bad is it?" I asked.

"Uhhhhhh," Rog groaned.

"Maybe just a titch more detail?"

"Uhhhhhh. Arg," Rog said helpfully.

He lay face down, his face buried in a cushion. I eyeballed his skinny form, seeing several small spots of blood on his shirt where it covered his middle. It didn't look so bad. I crawled over and carefully tugged the torn fabric away from his skin, grimacing. The skin beneath the bloody holes was pierced, each small hole already puffy and turning green. But the wounds were small. It could have been much worse. Rog had all his limbs, and they all seemed to be working. I stood up and grabbed him under the arms, tugging him off his face. "Sit on the..." I hesitated, realizing the couch wasn't usable. "Just lean against the couch and I'll go get something to put on those wounds."

Rog leaned his dark head back on the couch. He didn't respond.

"I'll be right back," I said, hoping to get a verbal response from him.

Nothing.

That wasn't good. Neither was the greenish tint that appeared to be quickly spreading over his body. Or the way his face had swelled.

That was the moment I realized that the tiny bites encircling his body weren't the real problem. It was whatever the teeth had infected the bites with.

And that looked serious enough to kill him.

8

SHADES OF MAGIC

P acing my room just wasn't getting the job done. I was a wreck, jittery and panicked, and nothing I did seemed to help.

I glanced toward my bed, where the covers barely mounded over Rog's too-still form.

At that moment, I would have given anything for some of the magic ointment Justice always used on me. But he'd refused to leave me a jar of it because he didn't trust me not to try to reverse engineer the stuff.

I should have tried harder to get some.

The thought that he didn't trust me was irritating. But not as irritating as it could have been, because I didn't believe he really felt that way. He was trying to make sure I continued to need him.

I sighed, dropping into the chair I'd pulled up next to the bed to oversee Rog's plunge into unconsciousness. His color hadn't improved and he'd been in a fitful sleep that I couldn't wake him from until about an hour earlier. Then he'd gone too still, his skin slimy with cold, greasy sweat.

I was losing him. And I had no idea what to do about it.

Justice had drilled into me that I should never take our special injuries to human medical personnel. But I was about ready to do just that. Maybe the poison that was making him sick wasn't magical. Maybe it was similar to puffer fish venom. Maybe they'd have an antidote.

Even as I had the thought I knew I was being ridiculous. The thing that attacked him hadn't come from our world. I doubted its venom would be anything human doctors had ever seen before.

I couldn't take him to a hospital. I needed to do something else.

There was only one option. And it wasn't a good one. Still, I needed to do it. I didn't really have a choice. But first, I was going to make sure I was prepared for whatever might happen. I had to change my clothes. I could barely stand to smell myself. Taking a three-minute shower, I towel-dried my short, curly hair and ran my fingers through it. Then I threw on jeans, a tee shirt with a fleece jacket over it, and a pair of comfortable boots. I slipped a blade into each boot and went to look for my gun. Which was when I realized I must have lost it when I'd plunged into the sea again.

I sighed. Knives it would have to be.

Hurrying back over to Rog, I threw back the covers and scooped him up, throwing him over my shoulders in a fireman's carry. Between his skinniness and the enhanced strength from the traveler magic coursing through my veins, I lifted him easily.

Then, taking a deep breath and closing my eyes to center myself, I thought about my destination. As the world righted itself again, a gust of wind slammed into me, nearly throwing me to the ground.

I cracked my eyes to look around at the wind-scoured

place. Aere. The air and wind dimension. And there, in the not-too-far distance, was the Travel Bureau. My destination.

I strode quickly toward the low, rounded structure. Before I'd gone halfway, the hobbit-style door in its center opened and three people ducked their heads and stepped out. My stride hitched uncomfortably as a moment of doubt assailed me. Would I not be welcome at the Bureau? I'd never come without Justice. Maybe they'd send me and my wounded cargo away.

A small man with a radical comb-over stepped forward as I came within ten yards of them. His dark eyes scanned my face, a question in their depths, then fell to Rog and narrowed. "Traveler Kitt. What's happened?"

His tone didn't have any of the warmth he'd offered when Justice and I had arrived there before. "I've lost my partners and this man was attacked by some kind of sea creature. I need your help."

Anil stared at me for a beat. Then, he said, "Lost? What do you mean, lost?"

I shifted Rog. Yeah, I was strong like bull, but he was starting to get heavy. "Do you think we could discuss this inside? He needs help."

Anil turned to the two people behind him. I recognized the woman with the frizzy orange hair and round, ruddy face. Her name was Fair and she'd helped me when I'd been injured in Aere before. I thought the man's name was Plant, or something gardeny. Names were unique in Aere.

"Please take our visitor to the clinic," Anil instructed, stepping back so Plant could take Rog from me.

As they started toward the door, Anil called out. "Allo?"

Ah. That was it. Aloe. I'd known it was something about a plant.

Allo turned back to us. "Yes?"

"Take care with the magic. That one's a null human."

Fair and Allo flinched, throwing twin worried looks toward Rog.

The first tinge of alarm sliced through me. "Is that a problem?" I asked Anil. "That he's human?"

"The fact that he's human is no concern. After all, you're human too. It's the fact that he's completely a-magical. We don't often encounter those." He frowned. "I'm afraid the bounce will have done him no good."

The trace of initial alarm doubled, twisting tightly in my belly. "What do you mean?"

Anil watched the door into the Bureau swing silently closed, a speculative look on his fleshy face. "I mean it might kill him."

I twitched violently. I couldn't kill Rog. If I did, my best friend would kill me. "You have to save him." Anil looked down at my hand clutching his arm. I hadn't even realized I'd grabbed him. I forced my fingers to relax. "He can't die."

Something in my voice must have reached him because he visibly softened. Patting me on the shoulder, Anil gave me a toothy smile. "We'll see what we can do." His teeth were shaped like jewelry pliers, with notches on the sides. I barely kept from shuddering. "Now tell me," Anil said, tugging me gently toward the door. "What has happened to Justice and Elvo?"

"Have you heard from them?" I asked, worry like acid in my gut.

"Several days ago, when Justice visited the armory and trained with Juggler. They generally train once a month or so."

I hadn't known that. Under the circumstances, that lack of knowledge felt like a betrayal. I should know more about my guide. Shouldn't I? Had I been too wrapped up in myself? In what the traveler gig was doing to my life? I realized I had been and vowed to change that if I got the chance.

Please heaven I'd get the chance.

Anil stopped at the door and turned to me. "Tell me what happened."

"We were called to Aqua. There was a portal in a ship. And rats." I shuddered. "Giant rats. Somehow they got through the portal, even though we thought we'd stopped them. And they took my friend, Molly." Tears threatened to fall and I blinked them back. I needed to keep my thoughts on the job at hand. If I gave in to tears, I'd be lost. "We were trying to find Molly. First Elvo disappeared, then Justice. We ran into Elvo again and he helped us with the rats. But then we were attacked by a sea monster of some kind."

"The Nessile." Anil shuddered. "Nasty creatures. Their venom is quite deadly."

I stared at him. In my befuddled state, I couldn't comprehend how he'd known that.

"I recognized the symptoms on the null," Anil explained. "They're quite unique."

I nodded, biting down on the fear his words inspired. "The thing had Rog and I couldn't think of anything to do. So, I bounced him away."

"You bounced him here," Anil said, not a question.

I shook my head. "To my apartment. Then, when I realized nothing I could do would help. I came here."

Anil looked appalled. "You bounced him twice?"

"Yeah...I... It was all I could think of." The look on his face made me want to slink away in shame.

He flapped a hand, impatient with me. "This is not a human hospital Traveler Kitt. You can't just bring everyone you know here to be magically healed."

Anger finally overcame my worry. "I can if they're

attacked by the magical world! It's not his fault he got pulled into this mess. He shouldn't have to die because of it."

Anil sighed. "Our jobs are not easy, Traveler. We must sometimes watch the weaker races succumb. But take comfort in the knowledge that, without us, they'd surely all succumb sooner rather than later."

"No."

He blinked in surprise. "What?"

"No. I won't take comfort in that. You forget I was just like them only a few weeks ago. In my mind, I'm still like them. You'll forgive me if I can't just wash my hands of them."

He expelled a frustrated breath and pulled the door open. "Come. We'll see if we can find your partners. If you want to save your friends, you'll need to stop whatever is hunting them."

Well duh.

I SAT in the semi-dark room staring at Rog's covers going up and down as he breathed. After several terrifyingly close calls where he'd stopped breathing altogether, I was just glad to see the covers moving at all.

I could barely stand to look at him. He had a deeply green tint to his brown skin and was puffed up like someone had put a ball pump into his mouth and kept pumping it. His eyes were so swollen he couldn't even open them, and his hands looked like latex gloves someone had inflated.

But the sound of his breathing was the worst. Wet and wheezy, each breath sounded as if it was his last. I wasn't even all that fond of the guy, but I'd been wiping tears of worry off my cheeks since entering the room. Guilt ate at me for having been fully healed of all my wounds while Rog fought for his life.

The door opened and I looked up to see Fair coming into the room. She had a large, flat bowl in her hands, and the liquid it contained glowed a pale red.

"Red?" I'd watched her apply a rainbow of magical concoctions to Rog's bloated form since plopping down in the chair. I'd been gathering key information about magic as she kept up a running conversation I suspected was meant to distract me from Rog's state.

"We're near the top of the magical scale now. Red is a top three hot color. Only orange and yellow are hotter."

I knew from our discussions that hot didn't mean heat. It referred to the level of magical power. The idea of magic still made me uncomfortable. I couldn't help feeling as if I'd hit my head and was hallucinating as I watched the ritual being repeated again.

Fair placed each of Rog's puffy hands in the liquid, one at a time, and waited a beat as the liquid flared to life, painting her features in ruby tones as it worked. Next, she placed each of his feet inside the bowl and the process was repeated. In the next step, she'd use a special sponge to wipe his body down with the liquid. Fair told me the sponge helped the magic sink more deeply beneath his skin, so it worked better. By the time she was done, Rog would glow like a lightning bug, looking like something that had been horked up by a nuclear reactor.

"As I told you," Fair said, her soft voice a soothing balm to my biting nerves as she worked. "Since he's a null, his tolerance for magic is very low. He'll need the strongest potions we have to survive this poisoning, but he would die if we used them on him. By easing him up the magical spectrum, we hope to enable him to eventually tolerate the strength we need to cure him."

She had told me that before, but I didn't mind her repeating it. Her unhurried, easy-going manner made the impossible seem feasible. I needed the reassurance after spending time with Anil.

His manner hadn't been at all reassuring.

As if I'd summoned him with my mind, Anil appeared in the open doorway, motioning for me to join him in the hall. I was strangely reluctant to leave the hard metal chair and stark medical suite behind, but I still had friends in danger and Anil was helping me figure out how to save them.

I stepped into a blindingly bright hallway that consisted of white tile floors, white stone walls, and white doors and fixtures. Aereons might have many useful attributes, but decorative genius didn't appear to be one of them. "What did you find?"

Anil handed me a small tube with unfamiliar symbols written along its length. "Take this to Douglass. He's the only one I have available right now. If Kimmie gets free in the next couple of hours, I'll send her to you."

Kimmie was a fellow traveler. She'd worked with Justice as her guide well before I came along. For several reasons, the attractive redhead wasn't one of my favorite people. And, after I'd bounced over her during one of my initial assignments, I had a feeling I wasn't one of her favorites either.

I ran a fingertip over one of the symbols. It looked like a crescent moon with echoes of itself pulsing across the container. The vessel looked like cardboard, but felt like polished wood. The symbol appeared smooth and felt like sandpaper. "Does Juggler know I'm coming?"

Anil grimaced. Apparently he wasn't fond of Doug's nickname. I had to agree it wasn't very dignified. Especially since it was based on his tendency to shamelessly juggle the women he dated.

"How are we going to find them?" I asked, wondering what the strange tube had to do with it. "And what am I doing with this?" I held the vessel up between us.

"*You* won't be doing anything with that. Give it to Douglass. He'll know what to do."

"Maybe you could tell me so I'll learn?" My tone held irritation, though I'd really tried to rein it in. I was getting sick of being treated like an idiot.

Anil sighed. "I know this is frustrating, Traveler Kitt. I assure you, I'm not trying to be difficult. It's just that we've only got a small window to find and save your partners. You need to hurry."

My spidey senses flared. "What about my friend Molly?"

Anil gave me a kind smile. "If you can talk Douglass into locating her after you find the others, you'll find her."

Anger joined the frustration and fear clawing through my chest. "And if I can't?"

Anil reached out and squeezed my arm. "You remember where he lives?"

I bit down on the scream dancing on my tonsils and nodded, my lips a straight, tight line.

"Good. I do wish you well on your journey, Traveler Kitt. Rest assured, we'll do all we can to help your null friend while you're away."

9

TIME FOR THE BIG GUNS

Douglass Prince lived in a small house built under a grass-topped mound of dirt. In Aere, those who had the means lived in underground homes to protect them from the wind's deleterious effects. Those who didn't faced every day not knowing if they would survive. The wind was well known to Aereons. But it was also well feared.

The front door of Juggler's underground home was painted a stark white and had three rectangular windows across the top and long windows on either side. Those windows were likely the only source of natural light in the entire house.

Around the mound, a veritable graveyard of broken and battered trees proved what a powerful force of nature Aere's wind was.

The man who opened the white door after I knocked appeared to be in his thirties, though I'd learned from Justice that appearances in the other dimensions were deceiving. Justice was apparently over three hundred years old, and he looked even younger than Juggler.

The man's expressive gray gaze widened when he spotted me, and he ran long fingers through chin-length, gleaming black hair as he leaned against the doorframe and slid an appreciative gaze from the top of my head to my toes. "Traveler Kitt. What a pleasant surprise. I don't suppose you've come to take me up on my offer?"

I frowned. "What offer?"

He placed a hand over his heart and pretended to swoon. "You don't even remember my proposition? I'm devastated."

When I stared at him, brows raised, he laughed. "I guess it's not too surprising. After all, I did stab you and leave you for the monsters to gather up."

"Yes," I agreed, my gaze narrowing. "You did do that."

He barked out a laugh and grabbed me, pulling me in for a hug that made my bones creak. "Come on in. Anil told me what's going on. If we're going to get to them before they're killed, we're going to need to hurry."

Well, I thought. *That isn't terrifying at all.*

I followed him into the house, which was just as I remembered it, except a little messier. The main room had a low ceiling and was lit only by the windows in front and a fireplace which took up most of one wall. If I was a betting woman, I'd wager that fireplace heated the whole house, since living underground likely made the temps fairly moderate no matter what they were outside the structure. The fireplace danced and crackled merrily, the trace of woodsmoke turning the dimly-lit room cozy.

Juggler shoved a pile of clothing off one of two chairs in front of the fire and indicated that I should sit. "Would you like something?"

I shook my head. "No. Thanks. I'm good."

He nodded and cleared a spot in the second chair,

lowering himself into it. "Tell me what's happened. From the beginning."

I quickly ran through our attempt to stop the rat things from getting through the portal, the subsequent discovery that the threshold led to The Muddle's backyard, and that Molly was missing. "Her assistant, Rog, insisted on coming along to rescue her." I said, grimacing. "Unfortunately, he was stung...or bitten...by some kind of sea monster and he's in bad shape."

Juggler nodded. "Anil told me about the Nessile. That was a bit of bad luck, for sure." He looked contemplative for a moment. His gaze sharpened. "Tell me about the place where you saw this shack."

I shrugged. "I didn't see much. There was a shoreline, a lot of fog, and three moons."

He lifted a pair of dense black brows. "Three? Are you sure?"

I nodded and he sighed. "You were dumped into a sub dimension. That's not good."

"What does that mean?"

Juggler stood up and began to pace in front of the fire. I admired how the warm colors of the flames caressed his strong, angular features and highlighted the midnight hues of his hair in gold. "What do you know about Aqua?"

"Not much. Justice told me that of the four main dimensions it was the one least likely to require our services."

Juggler nodded. "That's true. But, did he tell you why that was?"

I shook my head. "Not specifically. I'd assumed it was just more stable than the other dimensions. Or that water critters didn't seek other worlds so there was no danger they'd cross interdimensional boundaries to break into another dimension."

"That's true, as far as it goes. But not entirely the case. Because of its makeup, Aqua has no real hierarchy. Beneath the seas, it becomes a case of survival of the fittest. Everyone is hunter to some and prey to others. The Nessile is at the top of the food chain for many reasons. Some reasons are obvious...some less so."

I nodded. "Is it evil?"

He frowned. "Evil? Who's to say. Some would call us evil for our interference in the brutal and archaic paradigm of survival of the fittest. She's certainly a power to be reckoned with. And, since there's only one of her..." Juggler shrugged. "She mostly focuses on sustaining herself and her offspring. As long as you don't interfere with that, she'll generally leave you alone."

My eyes went wide. "She has offspring?"

"One. Nessiles only reproduce once in their long life-times." He waggled his brows at me. "It is said she appears in her human form to a humanoid male and seduces him."

"Imagine his surprise when she gives birth to a magical reptile."

He laughed. "That is unlikely, since her lover probably didn't live through the experience."

I winced. "She kills him?"

Juggler's expression was filled with delight. "Yep. Well, that's generally how it works out. I've heard of only one human who managed to escape a Nessile by swimming to a nearby ship and sailing away."

"Ugh."

"Ah," he said, shaking a finger at me. "But what a way to go."

"Pig."

He laughed. "Regardless, the main reason we aren't

called to Agua very often is that it really is uniquely uncontainable."

"Uncontainable? You're saying we can't keep them from breaking into the other dimensions?"

"From Agua, of course we can stop them. But there's more than one way to move from world to world in the water dimension. The most difficult to monitor and control is their ability to create sub-dimensions."

When I continued to look confused, he attempted to clarify. "Think of a bubble which has some of the characteristics of the main world, but is not held within a particular boundary." He seemed to consider his words for a beat and then added, "Like a dirigible flying above the surface of two worlds...able to move into one from another."

My eyes went wide. "That's..." the sheer horror of that thought turned me speechless. What if that Nessile thing got into the ocean on Terro?"

"I see you understand how bad this is."

I wasn't sure I did, fully. "How do we access this subD?"

Juggler sighed. "That, my beautiful friend, is the problem. How does one enter a dirigible in flight?"

"We could bounce," I offered, having no other suggestions to give.

"I'm afraid that's not possible. We can only bounce to a place we've been called to, or one we can picture in our minds. When you add in the fact that the dirigible is always moving, the chances of successfully bouncing to it are miniscule."

"Then what?" I asked, desperation clear in my voice despite my trying to keep it neutral.

He sighed. "You're not going to like it."

"I'm sure about that, since I haven't liked anything about this mess so far."

Juggler stopped pacing and pinned me with a look. His usually playful gaze was about as far from teasing as it could be. "We have to backtrack to find where you entered the sub-dimension."

That didn't sound so bad. "Okay. Let's go. I'm guessing it was the fog outside of The Muddle."

He was shaking his head before I finished my sentence. "No. You were already deep inside it at that point. Earlier."

That was when it hit me. I didn't even realize my head was shaking as I spoke. "No. Not a chance."

"It's the only way," he said, the first glint of mischievousness flaring through his gray gaze.

"You can't be serious! No. I told you, we came through the portal and back to Terro. We were in the real world when we found Rog."

"No. You weren't."

He was really starting to irritate me. "How do you know that?"

He dropped into his chair, leaning forward and propping his muscular forearms on his thighs. His gaze locked on mine. "The scene you walked into…did it feel normal? Or was there a sense of the surreal? A feeling that something didn't feel quite right?"

My gaze broke from his, so I wouldn't have to look into his knowing eyes. I looked everywhere but at him, fighting the urge to jump up and run away so I didn't have to face the truth.

"Rae?"

"Argh!" I exclaimed with heat. "How?"

"I told you, the sub-dimension overlays both dimensions. It is part of your world now."

"Then why can't we just go back to Molly's store and enter it?"

"It doesn't exist on a physical level there."

"Then how did Justice and I walk right into it before?"

Juggler shrugged. "Maybe you stepped into a magical swale. I don't know. Or, if the creature who took Molly wanted you to cross there, you could have. But without an invitation, we'll have to return to that ship on Aqua to enter."

I knew he was right. I could feel it in my bones. But Jeezopete in a leotard, I really didn't want to do it.

He grinned widely, the expression strange and irritating under the circumstances. "Now. I believe Anil gave you a vial?"

I handed it to him. "What is it?"

He winked and pulled a flat bowl closer on the table. "Why it's magic, Traveler Kitt."

I gave him a look. "What does the magic do, Douglass Prince?"

He held the vial above the bowl and closed his eyes, his lips moving but no sound coming forth. Without warning, he broke the vial and dumped a shimmering golden substance into the bowl. Then he held out a hand. "Your hand, please."

I frowned. "Why?"

Instead of explaining, he simply wiggled his fingers.

I sighed, giving him my hand.

"You must set the spell," he told me. "I was not present the last time you were called there."

I bit down on a plea not to go back. If there was a single place in all the universe I never wanted to visit again, it was that stupid, rat-infested ship. But it appeared I wasn't going to have a choice in the matter.

He gave me a mischievous look. "Ready?"

I opened my mouth to say no, just as he slapped my hand into the dish.

The world twisted and bent, and my heart started to rocket beneath my ribs.

10

RATS! AGAIN?

I wasn't prepared. I really should have been. But I wasn't. Juggler and I splashed down in the belly of the ship and sank to the soggy wood floor. As I pushed off to return to the surface, I felt the violent churn of the liquid around me and battled the debris from broken crates and splintered wood, along with the bloated carcasses of the rats Justice and Elvo had killed.

As I burst into the shallow layer of air, I was immediately assailed by flailing furry limbs and slashing claws. More rats. Ugh! It took me a beat to realize the half dozen rats I counted weren't attacking, they were simply trying to survive as the water level continued to rise.

I'd have felt badly for them, except that they were nasty and, if they managed to reach the portal ahead, they'd be infesting my world.

At least that was the theory. Despite my previous experience, I would believe that gaping, swirling black hole at the end of the ship led home once I saw it with my own eyes. But then, I realized, it didn't really. Did it? It led to a subD that apparently overlaid Terro.

I was so confused.

The stench of fear and destruction fouled the remaining air, along with something else I couldn't identify.

Something smacked my shoulder and I turned, my knife hand coming up to slash at my attacker. But it wasn't an enemy...or at least not totally...it was Juggler trying to catch my attention. When I looked where he was pointing, my eyes went wide.

Oh, oh!

It was just a thin membrane of blue flame when we spotted it. But it spread quickly, oozing like burning oil across the dryer wood of the ceiling. It ran down the hull near the stern and painted a floating barrel near the back of the ship. By the time it dipped into the black water where we struggled against the tide, seemingly not deterred by the fact that it was liquid, Juggler and I were slashing our way frantically toward the portal.

Around us, the rats became frenzied, telling us better than anything that the blue fire coming our way was exactly as deadly as we assumed.

We swam faster, slashing at any rats that got in our way. Unfortunately, they'd turned zombielike in their panic, seemingly not even feeling the deadly bite of our knives.

The air behind us ignited with a low-pitched whoosh, bathing the belly of the ship in pulsing blue flame as it rushed to fill the space.

I jammed my blade into the shoulder of a particularly large white rodent and used it like a pylon to pull myself past. The thing squealed and I turned, feeling bad for causing it needless pain, and felt my lungs lock down as I watched the thin, blue layer of flame expunge the creature from the tail forward, like a child wielding a giant blue eraser on a stick figure.

That was no ordinary fire.

No more Ms. nice gal. With a growl, I punched and slashed and savaged my way past the frantic rodents. I managed to stay, just barely, ahead of the blue flame, but it was only a matter of time until it took me down.

"Rae!"

My head shot up and I spotted the hand Juggler was offering me. He was crouched on the back of a frantically swimming rodent, and I didn't hesitate for a second to accept his offering. I grabbed his hand as more squealing went up behind us.

As soon as my feet hit the monster's thickly furred back, we started to run, leaping off the rodent's head and onto the next creature in line.

Still, we were barely staying ahead of the blue extinguisher. The monster we were using for a runway disintegrated underneath us and we had to leap to the next in line before we were prepared. Juggler landed on his left foot and wobbled, his momentum not enough to send him forward onto the next beast's back.

"Rae!" he screamed, and I barely got hold of his flailing arm to keep him from falling into the deadly churn below us. I yanked him hard and he stumbled into me. The beast below our feet started to scream.

We took off running, feeling the heat of the blue fire nipping at our heels even as the unfortunate creature beneath us disappeared, one furry inch at a time. The portal loomed up in front of us, roiling, dark, and terrifying. But nothing was as terrifying as the magical fire extinguishing everything around us. So, we clutched each other's hands and, less than seconds ahead of the flames, leaped with everything we had, praying we'd be in time.

The seconds slowed to hours.

The events around me lost focus, blurring into a kaleido-scope of motion and sound. My right foot launched me off its furry support, my left leg stretching toward the portal.

Juggler was a heartbeat ahead of me, his long, black hair lifted and his jaw tense as he leaped toward the terrifying nothingness.

There was a jerk on my arm as he disappeared. Agony bit at the back of my heel. And then I was inside the black nothingness, and the stench of the sea was gone.

I hit the ground hard, crying out with pain as my foot landed and then yelping again as my ankle twisted under impact.

A nearby grunt told me Juggler had landed too, but we'd somehow lost hold of each other in the passage.

I rolled to my back and lay there panting. As before, I was dry, but still felt as if I were covered in the salt residue the briny water had left behind. I panted for a beat, trying to ignore the pain in my left heel.

Then Juggler shifted, sending a few small rocks my way. "You okay?"

I thought about his question for a beat and then sighed. "Mostly."

Footsteps cut the distance between us and he stopped, looking down at me. "Want to do it again?" His handsome face was alight with excitement. "That was a hoot."

I got to my elbows, groaning softly. "You're certifiable." I took the hand he offered and sat up, taking it slow. "What was that blue stuff?"

"We call it Blue Obliteration. It's what happens when a subD outlives its usefulness."

"It self-destructs?" I asked, examining the painful spot over my heel.

"Pretty much."

I shook my head. "I'm really starting not to like Aqua."

He barked out a laugh. "It's definitely interesting."

"Is anything real here?"

He seemed to consider my question for a beat and then frowned. "Can I get back to you on that?"

I pulled my injured leg across my other thigh and looked at it. "Yikes."

He bent closer. "Is that what I think it is?"

"If you think that stuff ate the back of my shoe and licked my heel, then yes."

"That's cutting it a bit close, Rae."

I gave him a look. "If I hadn't had to save your butt..."

The smile on his face widened. The guy was hopelessly unserious. "We should get going," he said, but I held up a finger. "I came prepared this time," I told him. Reaching into my jeans' pocket, I removed the small tube of salve I'd stolen from the Bureau when I'd been sitting with Rog.

Juggler laughed when he saw what it was. Ignoring him, I squeezed out more than I probably needed and slathered it over the burned skin of my heel. Instant soothing followed and I sighed. "I need vats of this stuff."

"You humans sure do get hurt a lot."

I smacked his arm and swung around, intending to start at The Muddle like before. But we weren't at the muddle. The portal had dumped us out in a different spot. I swore softly.

"What's wrong?" Juggler asked, his gaze sliding over the misty shoreline.

I sighed. "Nothing. I just thought I'd have a few minutes to work up to this. I eyed the shack on the long dock and, in the distance, the rolling hump of a giant sea creature, whose hostile regard I could almost feel scraping along my skin."

"Well then," Juggler said. "Let's go."

I reluctantly fell in beside him and we moved quickly toward the shack in the distance. I kept one eye on the water alongside the dock, seeing the shadows moving through the dark liquid and tasting genuine fear on the back of my tongue. Movement in the distance drew my gaze back out to sea, where the Nessile still cut a lazy path across the horizon.

I didn't trust that distance. She'd appeared too suddenly before and Rog had paid dearly for her unreasonable speed. Still, we'd nearly reached the front door of the shack and the Nessile was still gliding peacefully across the distance.

The tortoise was in the same spot as before. Its almond-shaped black eyes watched us approach, but the creature didn't show any signs of hostility.

"Hello there," Juggler said, crouching down to look into the creature's face. To my surprise, he reached into his pocket and pulled out some kind of red fruit, offering it to the tortoise on his palm.

To my surprise the creature took the fruit carefully off Juggler's hand, chewing it thoughtfully. When the fruit was gone, the tortoise turned around slowly, its thick limbs moving stiffly and its claws scratching against the wood of the dock. Reaching the edge, the creature gave one last clumsy shove with its claws and fell into the water, disappearing from sight.

I stared at Juggler in shock.

When he saw my expression, he laughed. "He's the gatekeeper. You have to pay the gatekeeper."

I had a face-palm moment. I'd been so stupid.

Juggler dropped a heavy arm around my shoulders. "Don't beat yourself up, Traveler. You don't know what you don't know."

Shrugging out from under his arm, I glared at him. I was

a cop, not a suburban housewife. I should have known better. Clearly the turtle was there for a reason. I'd assumed the reason was as some type of deterrence. I should have taken it to the next logical step. Bribery is always the optimum first offer to avoid unnecessary violence. My jaw tight, I asked, "Is the Nessile in on the deal?" A quick glance out to sea told me the creature hadn't moved any closer.

Juggler's gaze followed mine. He grinned. "Nah. She's just got a special taste for non-magic humans."

"Great," I murmured. "My ignorance is going to get me and everybody around me killed."

His grin widened. "Nah. Just don't hang out with non-magics and you'll be fine."

11

THIS LITTLE PIGGY GOES TO MARKET

I jerked to a halt just inside the door, my gaze sliding over the scene spread out before me. And I do mean spread out. The space was enormous. As if carved from the inside of a mountain, the walls were rough-hewn stone. The floors were terraced, reminding me of fungi clinging to a tree.

I stood on the uppermost terrace, the rest of the space spreading out below me on dispersed levels of terracing. Juggler's big body crowded me on the small landing where we stood, urging me forward without words. But I couldn't stop staring at the sight below us.

Hundreds of creatures moved busily from booth to booth, many humanoid but more than a few looking like they'd escaped the pages of a fairy story.

A soft sound had me spinning around and I gasped, finding the door we'd entered through gone.

Juggler scanned the massive space below. "You didn't think getting out again would be that easy, did you?"

"Silly me," I murmured. "What is this place?"

"An inter-dimensional market. I'd heard of them, but I've never seen one before."

"I'm guessing it's another sub-dimension?"

"Yep." He pointed to an area on the far side, where several small, delicately made creatures with multi-hued butterfly wings spun and dipped through trees leafed in pinks, purples, and golds, dancing for an audience of mostly men sitting on tree trunks around them. Light, ethereal-sounding music drifted upward from the scene, the sound so rich and vibrant we could have been standing right next to it. "They're doing the fairy dance," Juggler said with awe in his voice. "I thought that was just an urban legend."

I frowned at the sight. It reminded me too much of a strip club for me to find it charming.

Booths built from live trees or parts of trees dotted each terrace. Fabrics in all weights and patterns adorned one booth, and brightly colored goods were being sold alongside a wide assortment of exotic food offerings.

The earthy scent of animals drew my gaze to a series of fenced off areas holding what I could only assume were farm beasts. Some of them bore a vague resemblance to pigs, but the single large, curved horn on their furry pink heads was decidedly un-pig-like.

Behind the fenced areas, a long, narrow platform ran the length of the space, the pale wood dotted with dark stains that made my stomach twist with dread.

"This is as good a place as any to find Molly," I told Juggler. The thought made my stomach churn with nerves.

He nodded and pointed toward the spot where the pigs butted heads and snorted, their antagonistic behavior another factor that made them unlike pigs from home. "The auction is our best bet," Juggler said. "If they brought her here, that's where they'll hold her. There are reinforced cages in the caverns behind the auction."

I didn't like the sound of that. And eyeing the half dozen men in rough tan uniforms and carrying weapons of some sort, I didn't like our chances either. My blade wouldn't do much good against a gun. "What about Justice and Elvo?" I asked.

"They won't be together. If he located her, Justice will be near the girl. Elvo's strength is his ability to stay out of sight, stalking and assessing the situation for the right moment to strike."

A tiny string of hope threaded through me. "So Elvo could be somewhere in the market?" I tightened my gaze on the shadowed places down below.

"It's likely, yes."

"How will we find him?"

"We won't," Juggler said. "He'll find us when the time is right. In the meantime, let's make a pass through the place and get a feel for it."

I'm only slightly ashamed to admit my mouth was hanging open as we descended into the market, heading toward a colorful stand I'd spotted from up top.

We dodged around "people" who were literally all shapes, sizes, and colors. I nearly got stepped on by a purple-skinned creature with white hair, a wispy white beard, and nearly iridescent blue eyes. The creature was so tall, it took him or her several seconds to scan a look down at me and apologize in a language I couldn't understand.

"Aero giantess," Juggler said in a low voice. "Royalty. They're very polite but their eyesight isn't great."

I shook my head, staring rudely after the enormous woman. The giantess moved in long, slow strides that, despite her size, made very little sound as she walked.

A strident squeal yanked me out of my reverie and I had my blade in my hand as I spun toward the sound.

"Stop it!" someone screamed, as one of the horned pig things galloped toward us, its beady black eyes fixed on me as it lowered its head, pointing the oversized horn right at me.

Juggler glanced at my blade and shook his head. "If you kill it, you'll have to buy it. And you don't have the kind of money that would cost. Igne currency is measured in platinum."

I had so many questions. But the pig shot forward as if blasted from a cannon, and I barely had time to spin aside to avoid being skewered.

The pig shot past, its enormous hooves slicing across the leather of my flat, black, leather boots. I spun again as it leaped off the ground, twisted in the air and jabbed at me with its horn.

I mentally added unusual agility to the differences between the pigs of home and the pigs of Igne.

"Jeezopete!" I yelled. "What's this thing got against me?"

Juggler stood aside, hands in pockets, grinning like an idiot. "I don't know, but this is fun."

"Bite me!" I yelled. "Help me keep this thing from goring me with that enormous, flippin' horn."

Juggler looked like he was considering my demand. "I don't know. You're doing so well on your own."

I dodged sideways again and the pig leaped into the air, its fat body twisting impossibly to come down facing me, horn locked on target. With a squeal, the thing struck. With nowhere else to go, I swung around, hoping it would miss.

Pain lashed across my right buttock as the thing's horn sliced me on the way down.

It hit the ground, propelled itself back into the air, and

spun to come at me again. I yanked my blade free of its sheath. "That's it. This thing's bacon."

Four enormous split hooves left the ground. A wide slash opened in the pig's ugly face, showing teeth that belonged on a wolf rather than breakfast on hooves. And my weapon came up, blade braced in two hands. "Come and get me pork-pie."

The thing made a snorfling kind of noise and actually smiled, its horn aimed right at my heart.

I braced.

The pig lowered its head.

I growled.

An enormous arm appeared between me and the flying pig. The thing crashed into the hairy limb, which was as big around at the forearm as my thigh.

The pig crashed to the ground and the man attached to the arm landed on top of it. Both creatures grunted upon impact.

With nothing to stop my forward momentum, I stumbled and nearly landed on top of them. Only Juggler's hand on my arm stopped me from falling. He yanked me back and leaned close enough to whisper. "We've got to move."

I jerked my arm from his grip. "Thanks so much for the help."

"You're welcome."

Did nobody from Aere understand sarcasm?

He was moving fast, forcing me to jog to keep up. I shook violently, crashing from the adrenaline overload the pig fight...I'd never imagined ever saying those words...had caused. I was panting and tired. "Hold up, let me catch my breath."

He shook his head. "No time. While you were dancing with piggy, our friends arrived."

I glanced around, huffing and puffing as I struggled to keep up. "What friends?"

He stopped, caught my eye, and slowly slid his gaze toward a nearby fruit stand.

Mean pink eyes peered directly at us. An enormous, hairy man stood between us and any chance of escaping in that direction. His eyes were small and round and his mustache stuck straight out to the sides, like whiskers. Thick gray hair covered his arms and chest beneath the plain gray shirt. He smiled meanly and his teeth were over-sized, the middle ones square.

He was a rat in human form. The intensity of his gaze told me he probably wasn't looking to make friends.

We spun around and jolted to a stop. Another rat-man, slightly smaller than the first with light-brown hair, stood on the walkway we'd taken from above. There was a third man blocking our path toward the terraces on our right.

Leaving only the path toward the auction pens open.

My gaze lifted to Juggler's and he gave me a shrug. Outwardly, he seemed unconcerned, but I saw the tightening around his serious gray eyes. "I guess we're going this way," he said loudly.

We started walking, awareness prickling along my back as the three rat-like men watched us leave. I put a hand on the hip sheath that held my blade.

Juggler put his hand over mine. "Not here."

Though I nodded, I kept my hand on the blade. "Why do I think those men are familiar with the rats from the ship?"

"Shifters," he said, his gaze scanning the area, probably to assess our options like I was doing. "From Igne."

The monster dimension. "Makes sense."

Juggler nodded. "Look around. What do you see?"

I scanned the area around us and noticed that we moved through open space where moments earlier, shoppers had filled the walkways and buzzed around the stands. Even the uniformed security guys with guns were gone.

A muscular, dark-haired man hurried past, his fingers wrapped around the hand of a golden-haired little girl. The man avoided my gaze, his movements fast and jerky, bordering on panic. The little girl gave me a smile, her clear blue gaze unconcerned by whatever had made her parent tense.

A roar filled the sudden silence and everyone stopped.

My gaze caught on the little girl's, I was surprised she didn't jolt in fear. Instead, she slid a glance slowly toward a tall, narrow shadow in the wall directly to our left, just behind a booth that sold bolts of rough, brown fabric and strange hats that drooped around the face of the manikin wearing it, all but obscuring her features.

The roar sounded again. I realized it came from the caverns behind the auction stage.

A softly cleared throat brought my gaze back to the girl. She'd halted her concerned parent and stood smiling at me. The child nodded toward the long shadow. "Go," she said softly.

"We need to get out of here," Juggler said, his customarily jovial manner gone. "That's a bear. If it's from Igne..."

He never finished the sentence, because the shadows behind the stage shifted and stretched, belching out the biggest bear I'd ever seen. And once its small black eyes locked onto us, it never looked away.

"I guess we found your friend's bear," he said.

12

BUMBLES BOUNCE

"Come on!" Juggler yelled.

I jerked away from his grip, unwilling to leave the little girl alone. "Wait, we need to help..." But when I looked back their way, the little girl and the man were gone. I glanced quickly around the market but didn't see them anywhere.

"Rae!" Juggler urged. "We need to go!"

The bear was no more than twenty feet away, its massive paws making soft, thumping sounds in the dirt of the market floor as it ran. It opened its huge maw and roared again, the sound encasing my spine in ice and bringing gooseflesh popping up along my arms.

My fight or flight instincts kicked in heavily on the side of flight. I didn't even make the conscious decision to run. I just turned toward the shadow on the wall and took off.

Juggler was hot on my heels.

I stumbled on a tree root and fell into the fabric stand, my hands clutching a bolt of material as I fell.

Juggler reached for my arm and tugged hard enough to wrench my shoulder. Saturated in adrenaline, I barely felt the pain. I shoved against the ground and let the impetus from his pull get me on my feet.

Another roar actually vibrated the air around us. Juggler and I whipped around to find the creature standing five feet away, on its back legs, slobber running from its stained teeth and foul breath blowing the hair back from my face.

My heart thumped against my ribs. The creature roared again, its claws scratching against the wooden sides of the stand and shaking it so hard the cross bar at the top that had been holding the vendor's sign, fell off and hit the ground behind the structure.

The bear's body tensed and I knew it was going to move.

Without thinking, I grabbed Juggler's hand and pictured the terrace above our heads. The world shifted around us and we landed hard, falling over a tree stump and nearly toppling over the edge. Juggler caught the stump and managed to yank me to a stop before we fell. Gasping, I shoved to my feet. "Well, that was clo..."

Another roar had me jumping to my feet.

My head snapped around. The monster was six feet away from Juggler and closing fast. With a yelp, I did the only thing I could do. I grabbed Juggler again and sent the world spinning away one more time.

As my feet hit the ground, I opened my eyes to a darkness so complete I thought I'd gone blind.

"Where in the goddess's crooked big toe are we?" Juggler asked.

I grimaced, barely able to see his outline only a foot or so away from me. The walls were rough and close, and a wave of claustrophobia swept through me, leaving me damp with a cold, oily sweat. Swallowing hard, I said, "It looked much bigger when she showed it to me."

"What looked bigger?" His voice held a suggestive edge, as if he thought I was offering a raunchy joke.

"The crevice," I responded, irritated. Only a man could think about sex at a time like thi...

Something massive slammed into the entrance wall and the thin ribbon of light disappeared, casting us into complete darkness. Another wave of panic sliced through me, and my pulse skyrocketed. We crouched, arms over our heads as rocks and dust filtered down on us.

I felt as if I might stroke out.

"Roar!!"

"How is that thing sticking with us so closely?" I mumbled to myself.

"Bumbles bounce," Juggler said, a smile in his voice.

Honestly, the man took nothing seriously. "Can you please focus for a minute. We're fighting for our lives here." *And for the lives of my partners and friend*, I added in my mind.

"I *am* focusing. That type of bear has transport magic. He gloms onto our bounce trail and follows it."

"That's just awesome." I ran my hands over my sweaty face and rubbed them on my jeans. "What now?"

Juggler shifted as the crevice rumbled under another assault from outside. "Now, we follow this tiny crack in the wall and see where it takes us." When I just stared at him, not responding or moving, he added, "Honestly, Rae, this crevice was genius. The bear can't follow us in here. It's too small a space. Let's take advantage of that. I have a hunch this leads into the auction caverns. With any luck we'll find Justice and your friend."

I expelled a sigh, fighting the panic that was robbing me of air. I'd always been a little afraid of tight spaces. But I'd never known sheer terror like I was currently experiencing.

Bam, bam, bam!

More rocks fell, a sharp one gouging the top of my head. I knew Juggler was right. We needed to keep moving. And the only option we had was to move more deeply into the crevice. Worst case, we'd get deep enough inside that the bear couldn't smell us anymore. Maybe it would lose interest and go away.

I sighed. "Okay. Let's do it." I turned around and fully intended to take the first step. But my feet didn't seem to want to move.

A moment later, Juggler squeezed past and grabbed my hand. "Come on. I'll let you buy me a beer when this is over." He pulled out one of those tiny, really skinny clear devices that I assumed were Aere's version of the cell phone and tapped the surface. A decent flare of light illuminated the area around us.

Better. My chest loosened a tiny bit. Still, a beer sounded good. Really. Good. And I didn't even drink.

My phone rang through the absolute darkness a few minutes later. I looked down at the screen, seeing my daughter's name. I closed my eyes, suddenly fighting tears. It seemed like weeks since I'd spoken to her. And several worlds away.

I pulled it out of the zippered plastic I'd encased it in for the trip through the sinking ship.

"Hey," I said, my voice tight with unshed tears. "How are you, baby girl?"

Silence met my question and I wanted to kick myself. "What's wrong, Mom?"

I tried to laugh it off but I could almost hear her frowning. "Nothing, honey. I'm just busy. How're things?"

"Good. But tell me what's wrong."

"Roar!!"

Rocks and dust filtered down on me. I hunched over my phone and curved an arm protectively over my head.

"What was that?" Elizabeth asked, sounding more than a little alarmed.

"It's just a movie. Jurassic Park. Love that T-Rex." Juggler gave me a look and I shrugged, motioning for him to keep moving. "Are you staying out of trouble?" I asked, more than a little aware of the hypocrisy of my asking.

"Of course not. Where's the fun in that?"

I smiled, warmth infusing me at the happy sound of her voice. "Well then good...I guess. Have you heard from your dad lately?" My kid's dad and I had been divorced for several months, and he still called me once in a while, but there was no going back for us. He had promised me that he'd remain a part of our only child's life.

"We're going out to dinner tonight. He's taking me to Zaggby's. That new burger joint? I heard their chicken sandwich is to die for."

I bit back a sigh. The man always had been cheaper than a plastic suit. "That sounds delicious." I wasn't lying. My stomach growled at the thought of it, and I realized I hadn't eaten for a while. "How's work going?"

As usual, Elisabeth was happy to talk about her work as a nurse in an ER unit. The kid was scarily good at diagnostics. Anywhere but on Terro her skill would probably have been classified as near magical. Regardless, it was a skill that was very helpful when treating people in an emergency situation. It sometimes made being her mother extra hard, however. But I was so proud of her.

"...he's super nice and I think he likes me."

I mentally flogged myself. I'd been woolgathering and had missed something important in Elizabeth's life. It sounded like she had a new boyfriend. "Of course, he likes you," I said, hoping she didn't ask me any specific questions about what she'd told me. "You're gorgeous, smart, and fun. You have to beat potential beaux off with a stick. The question is, do you like him?"

"Beaux, mom?" She laughed happily. "Sometimes you sound like you were transplanted from the eighteen hundreds."

If she only knew.

Juggler stopped without warning and I ran into him with an "oomph!" sound.

"Mom?"

"Ah. I stubbed my toe. You know I can't walk and talk at the same time."

She giggled.

I glared at Juggler, but he couldn't see it in the dark. Moving up beside him, I realized the wall had finally opened. We'd reached the end of the crevice. And my kid had distracted me from going fetal on the hard dirt floor with claustrophobia.

The cavern we were staring into was much better lit than the crevice had been, And it was full of cages. Most of them were empty but...

I gasped.

"Mom?"

I realized she'd been talking to me while I'd been focused on the man sprawled bonelessly across the floor of the nearest cage. I stared at the dark stains covering his bare arms and torn clothing. From where we stood, I couldn't see if he was breathing.

Justice!

"Mom what's wrong?"

"Nothing, sweet girl. I've got to go, okay. Work is calling.

But we're going to talk about your new friend again real soon. Okay?"

"Mom!" She tried to sound disgusted, but I heard the smile in her voice.

"Love you, honey." I managed to get her off the phone without...hopefully...creating additional worry that would end up in more questions about my new "job". My daughter was an intelligent woman who had strong protective instincts toward me. Instincts that had been forged through decades of never knowing if I'd return home at night when I'd been a cop.

She was my heart and soul. But she was safer not knowing anything about the traveler gig, which I couldn't possibly explain to her without earning myself a trip to a padded cell.

A distant roar reminded me that we had trouble behind and the terrifying quietness of my partner in that cage was a not-so-subtle reminder that we had more than enough problems ahead.

I had to focus.

"You have a daughter?"

I slid Juggler a quick, assessing look. "Not your business."

He shrugged. "I meant no harm. I was just going to say she's probably really strong."

I softened slightly, my pride getting the best of me for a beat.

"And pretty. Does she have a boyfriend?"

Instinct had me yanking my blade and placing it at his throat.

His gray gaze widened slightly, but then he grinned. "I guess a double date with you and Justice is out of the question?"

I growled. My hand tightened on the hilt of my knife.

Juggler didn't seem to notice the blood running down his muscular throat. "I'm just teasing, Traveler Kitt. Chillax, as the Terro youth say."

I stared into his eyes for another beat and then forced myself to step back. "Never mention my daughter again."

He shrugged.

"And Justice and I are not a thing."

His eyes twinkled, but he didn't respond.

I nodded toward my downed partner. "I'm going to try to get to him. Can you cover me?"

Juggler pretended to pull two six-shooters from his hips and fire them, blowing on his fingers, cowboy style.

I shook my head. "Just warn me if I get company."

I didn't wait for him to respond. Pressing my back against the rock wall, I slipped into the cavern, my gaze sliding left to right, forward and behind as I ran toward Justice's cage.

A soft whine jolted me to a stop. I knew that whine. "Elvo?" There was no sign of the big dog anywhere nearby, "Where are you, boy?"

Another whine. It sounded as if it came from the cage next to Justice's, but that cage was empty. I squinted, moving closer. "Or was it?"

A large black puddle shifted in the back corner and Elvo gave a little yelp of pain.

My rage came up in a big way. Kids and animals. I was a fool for both. My philosophy was that an adult who got him or herself into trouble due to their own choices, was one thing. I'd help them if I could. But kids and animals who'd been put into danger because of their reliance on someone else broke my heart.

I stopped in front of the cage. "Come here, Elvo."

Elvo started to stand, but jerked to a stop and flopped back down. The worst possibilities charged to the forefront of my imagination. Broken legs? Broken back?

A soft sound of concern escaped me, drawing an answering sigh from the big dog. My gaze slid to Justice. He was way too still, and I was torn. I could be discovered at any time and needed to move quickly. But they both needed me.

What should I do?

I needed more information. Taking a deep breath to battle back a jolt of fear for what I was about to do, I shoved away doubt and bounced. The short hop was surprisingly easy. But just to make sure...

I bounced out again, relief allowing me to breathe. The cage wasn't warded to keep me from bouncing. I quickly returned, hurrying over to Elvo as soon as my feet hit the ground inside his cage.

The big dog's tail gave one solid thump of greeting.

I crouched down next to him and placed a hand on one front leg. "Are you hurt?" I asked, feeling my way along the leg. He lifted his head and drenched the side of my face with a stinky kiss.

"Ugh," I murmured. "Dog slobber."

His tail thumped again and he slathered my arm with more spit. I lifted my shoulder to dry my face and sat back on my heels. "All your legs seem to be working." After a moment's consideration, I pulled out my phone. Keeping it close to the ground, I touched the screen and found the flashlight. A quick look with the light showed me the problem. They'd tethered him to a short, metal post that had been pounded into the ground. He couldn't stand or even shift very far. "Poor guy," I said, burying my face in his fur. "I'll get you out of here."

Unfortunately, the chain holding him was way too strong for my blade to break.

"What is it?" Juggler asked, his voice surprising me into a soft yelp. I glared at him. "He's chained. I can't break it."

Juggler suddenly appeared next to me in the cage. I jumped again, clutching my heart. "Give a girl some warning," I scolded.

He crouched down next to me, getting his own kiss of welcome from the vicious Hellhound. "Hold your light over the chain," he instructed.

I moved it to illuminate the place where the chain was attached to the post. He ran his hands over it a few times and then grunted softly, sitting back on his heels. "Okay, this is going to be tricky, but I think we can do it."

"Do what?" I scanned the too-quiet space, my heart thumping with worry.

"I'm going to send this pipe somewhere else. I need you to bounce Elvo outside the cage at the same time."

I frowned. "You sure that will work?"

"Nope." He stood and moved around behind Elvo, crouching to place a hand on the pipe. He glanced up at me. "Ready?"

"Is this safe for him?"

Juggler just stared at me. I wanted to argue. My mind spun trying to come up with another plan. Other than finding someone with the key and taking him down to get it, we were stuck. My stomach twisted with fear. "I don't like it."

Juggler's gaze still held mine, the silent message clear. We had no choice.

I sighed, placing one hand on Elvo's head and one on his body. "I'm ready."

"One..."

I looked into the dog's trusting brown eyes and felt my heart tear.

"Two..."

Elvo's eyes began to glow red.

I whipped around at the sound of a large, carnivorous creature snuffling and snorting as it made its way to us.

"Thr..."

"Wait!"

"...ee!"

The world jerked and tore. Beneath my hands, Elvo's big form was wrenched and I screamed as I changed the destination of my bounce at the last possible second.

We hung in oblivion for a beat and then slammed down hard on the dirt floor, barely missing the cage's other inhabitant.

I checked first to make sure we hadn't landed on Justice, and then ran my hands over Elvo to make sure he was whole and healthy. I didn't have a lot of time to check him out, though, because of the enormous bear slamming against the front of the cage we'd just entered.

13

BEARLY THERE

The cage shook so violently I thought for a moment it was going to topple over. The thick metal bars bent inward under the force of the massive bear's determined assault.

I tried to ignore it as I bent to make sure Elvo was okay. A large pink tongue slipped out and scraped my arm as I ran my hands over his fur. "Everything working?" I asked the big dog. In answer, he grunted softly and came to his feet, giving a full-body shake that ended with me getting whacked in the throat by his tail.

Spitting dog hair from my mouth, I crawled to Justice and placed a hand over the pulse point on his throat. It beat in weak but steady pulses. His skin was cool and I didn't like that, but I didn't see any wounds. I carefully turned him over onto his back, and yelped. His sapphire eyes stared at me, looking dazed.

"Rae?" he said, his voice rusty. "What are you doing here?"

"We're looking for you."

Elvo bumped into me, and a low growl rumbled against my back. I ignored him.

"Can you get up?"

He nodded, but fell back to the ground after an initial attempt.

"What happened?" I asked him, running my hands over his chest looking for a wound.

"Dosed," he mumbled in a voice that warned he was about to pass out again.

"Dosed with what?"

"Zombie juice."

I grimaced, hoping he didn't mean literal zombies. "Did you find Molly?"

Justice's chin rose a fraction in what I took as a nod. "She was here until a little while ago. Unfortunately, they had her well-guarded."

"A little help here, Rae!" a familiar, panicked voice called from the darkness beyond the cage.

My head whipped up and I searched the shadows for Juggler. A roar yanked me to my feet as I realized what must have happened. "Can you bounce?" I yelled into the shadows.

There was another roar, followed by a husky cry of pain. I ran to the front of the cage and pounded on it. "Come and get me, you overgrown teddy bear!"

The bear lumbered into sight, a dark liquid dripping from its maw.

"No!" I screamed. "Juggler!"

Silence met my terrified call. Then...

A tall shape emerged from the shadows, followed by two more men carrying a slumped and seemingly unconscious Juggler between them. The enormous, rat-like guys from the market had found us.

"Rae?"

I turned to Justice, torn between the two men. "Shh," I told him. "Stay still."

Elvo padded up next to me and dropped to his backside, a constant growl throbbing in his throat. As the men neared the cage, Elvo's eyes glowed a deeper red.

Sweat popped out on my face and trickled between my shoulder blades. I clutched the big dog's fur for comfort. "Let him go," I demanded of the men. We haven't done anything to you."

The bear padded off into the darkness, disappearing behind another row of cages. The largest rat-man stopped several feet away from the battered cage, eying Elvo.

I scrubbed my arm over my dripping face, nearly panting. When had the cavern gotten so hot?

"You must come with us," the man said.

"Not going to happen," I told him, lifting my t-shirt away from my sopping chest and flapping it to create a cooling breeze. The air was so hot it was more like a warm breeze.

The rat shifter took another step and Elvo lunged at the front of the cage with a snarl. The enclosure rattled and one of the door hinges broke.

I eyed it with alarm. At the moment, the cage was keeping us safe. Well, all of us except for Juggler. "Let him go and we'll let you live." Even I nearly grimaced at the threat. I had one irritated Hellhound mutt, one comatose guide, and another guide slash traveler who appeared to be unconscious and who was currently a prisoner.

Basically, I had Elvo and me.

They had numbers over us and a really big bear.

I needed to stall in the hopes that either Justice or Juggler joined the party. "Why do you want us to come with you?"

The rat-man wriggled his nose, his strange, whiskery mustache quivering. I barked out a laugh at the sight.

When he bristled, I held up my hands. "Sorry. Poor choice."

"You must come with us," he said again.

"Not a real creative speaker, are you?"

He stared at me.

"Hey," I asked, lightening my tone of voice. "You haven't seen a tiny, dark-haired woman, around here have you? She's about yay tall..." I held my hand about chest height. "If you gave her to me, I'd be happy to come with you. Call it a trade."

"You must come with us."

I expelled air. "You need to expand your vocabulary if you want to succeed in business."

The man moved much more quickly than I expected. Suddenly, he was attached to the front of the cage like a giant spider. He'd ripped the broken hinge away from the frame before I had time to blink.

By the time I managed to pull my knife, Elvo had already reacted. He flew at the rat-man, whose friends had dropped Juggler and were also attached to the front of the cage like bugs.

Light and heat flared into life. I left Elvo to his snarling attack and slashed at the rat-men's exposed flesh through the bars.

They barely seemed to notice when I sliced into their leathery palms or over-bendy legs. But when their friend ignited into a giant, red fireball with a blood-curdling scream, they noticed that.

I turned to find Elvo totally immersed in Hell fire, even his tail was aflame, wagging dangerously close to me in the constrained space.

"Whoa!" I yelled. "Keep that thing to yourself." I glanced at Justice, finding him still unconscious. "Hold the fort," I yelled at the dog. "I'll be right back."

With a thought, I bounced out of the cage and wrapped a hand around Juggler's ankle.

A blink later, we were inside the enclosure again. Wrapping my fingers around Justice's wrist, I glanced at the still-burning canine. "Douse yourself!" I yelled. "We need to get out of here."

The rat-men had the door nearly ripped free of the frame. We had maybe seconds before they were through.

Elvo whipped around and snarled at me.

I blinked in surprise.

I reached for him, but he snarled again, turning his attention to the creature climbing through the breach.

"He wants us to leave," Justice said, sounding drained.

"I can't leave him behind." I started to release the men but Justice turned his hand in my grip and grabbed me. "We'll come back for him, Rae. For now, we need to leave."

I was shaking my head, tears burning in my eyes, when the world hiccupped and shuddered, and we bounced out of the cavern. I collapsed as my feet hit the ground. The dirt beneath my knees stunk of rotted fish and was slimy with decayed seaweed. The smell made me nauseous.

Or maybe it was the fact that I'd deserted Elvo when he'd needed me.

A row of dilapidated buildings hung over us, their windows filthy and cracked, and their bones fractured in many places, broken into chunks of brick and mortar in others.

Casting my gaze out over the water, I had mixed feelings when I spotted the shack on the dock. The sight was both comforting, meaning that I hadn't traveled far from Elvo, and disconcerting, given that I had two injured men to protect until they regained their strength.

Someone groaned behind me. I mustered the strength to drop to my butt and turn toward the men. They were sprawled over the ground in a tangle of limbs. Justice was trying to sit up.

Juggler wasn't moving. I crawled over and felt his pulse. It took me several seconds to find it, which made my stomach twist with fear.

Justice appeared beside me. I looked up at his slack expression and drooping form. "I can't get a pulse."

His sapphire eyes widened slightly, energy seeming to stiffen his shoulders. "Let me try,"

I wanted to rail against his assumption that since I was a woman I must be doing it wrong. I'd experienced the phenomena too many times not to recognize it. But I bit my tongue, focusing on the most important thing. I watched him do the same thing I'd just done, biting my tongue to keep from sniping.

A moment later, he sat back on his heels. "You're right. His pulse is too weak to feel."

I did roll my eyes. But he didn't see it. "He's still breathing..." Barely. "We need to get him to the Travel Bureau."

Justice frowned. "I'd have to take him. That would leave you here alone. I'm not doing that."

"I'll be fine. You can get fixed up and then come back."

"No." He turned his frown on Juggler. "We'll put him inside. Try to give him some cover. The sooner we retrieve Elvo and find Molly, the sooner we can get out of here."

I would have loved nothing more than to get out of the goddess-forsaken subD. I'd had more than enough of rat-people, bouncing bumbles, stinky fish air, and magical markets.

Crossing my arms over my chest, I continued arguing. "Juggler will die if you don't take him."

"He'll be fine." Justice straightened, his movements stiff. "He's indestructible. Like a cockroach from Terro. You could stomp him into the ground and he'd just climb to his feet and walk away. Forget poison, he eats it for breakfast. You could shoot him with a silver bullet and he'd catch the bullet in his teeth and chew it to bits."

I fought a grin. "As colorful as that is, I don't believe a word of it." I pointed to the large, bloody gashes criss-crossing his stomach. "It appears rat-people claws are about to *destruct* him just fine."

Justice sighed. He stood, hands on hips, staring down at Juggler. "I hate to admit it, but you're right."

"Two in a row. I'm sensing a pattern."

Justice shook his head, but his sexy lips twitched. "I want you to promise me you'll take cover and wait for my return. I'll get back as fast as I can."

I opened my mouth to lie, but he placed a strong, warm finger over my lips. His sapphire gaze found mine and he lifted light-brown brows. "Don't bother to lie. The last time I left you to take this idiot for medical attention, you said you'd stay put and then marched right into trouble as soon as I left."

I grinned. "What's your point?"

"My point is..." He expelled a frustrated breath. "Never mind. Try not to get yourself killed."

I stepped back to give him room to scoop Juggler up and throw him over his shoulder. He fixed me with a last, surprisingly warm look before he turned away and strode off past the line of buildings, to the mist-shrouded area around the nearby street.

I waited only a beat to make sure he was gone. Then I

palmed my blades, pictured the auction cavern, and bounced.

14

OOPS!

My feet touched down with a splash and I jerked backward in surprise, my bare arm sliding over slimy rock. "Ew!" I exclaimed a little too loudly. Jerking away from a wet concrete wall, I gave a violent twitch and covered my mouth. Too late. I'd given myself away.

Something heavy shifted in the darkness, the sound of claws scrabbling against the slick floor. Without thinking, I started moving, keeping to the shadows and using the skeletal forms jutting from the floor up and the ceiling down to fracture my movements and hopefully confuse whatever was coming my way.

I feared it was one of those oversized rats and shuddered at the thought. Battling one of those nasty things was bad enough in the water when they were focusing most of their attention on getting to the portal. I really didn't want to face off with one on relatively dry ground.

Sweat coated my face and I had to keep drying my hands on my jeans so the blades I was clutching didn't slide through my fingers.

The air was thick, redolent with something dark and sinister. The fact that I couldn't see what was chasing me made it ten times worse. I was scared that by the time I did see the thing, it would be too late to get away.

Claws scratched against the ground, sounding much closer than they should have. A splash and a grunt, then the heavy sound of something moving through the quickly narrowing tunnel.

I shifted away from the noise, counting on the natural structures that looked like pitted and broken bone fragments to hide my flight.

Still, a beat later, the dense sliding sound was there again, always the same distance away. A rancid stench filled the underground space. A mix of feces, rotted vegetation and stale air thick with mildew. Every surface I touched was cold and slimy, like mucous from a giant slug.

I cracked my head on something and looked up to find the ceiling far too close. Then, spinning in a panicked circle, I realized the passage had shrunk to little more than the width of my outstretched arms.

Was I being herded? Was the passage going to end and I'd be trapped? And what about Elvo and Molly? I didn't even know if I was in the right place. No. I shook off the doubt. One thing I'd learned since being dumped into the magical world was that it had rules. I mostly didn't know any of the rules and they really didn't make much sense to me, but they were there.

I might have popped into a totally different sub-dimensional construct, but I had to believe I'd landed there for a reason. I had to believe I would find Elvo there. And Molly. Please goddess, let my best friend be there too. I couldn't shake the feeling that she was running out of time.

Icy water dripped from the curved ceiling of what could only be described as a sewer cavern. The bent and pitted protrusions around me resembled the ribcage of an ancient skeleton. I stood next to one of them and looked around, the sense that I was being funneled into a trap growing with every labored breath.

Swish.

I spun around, looking for the source of the sound. I saw nothing.

Swoosh.

I spun the other way, still seeing nothing.

A rock skittered over the ground behind me.

I turned more slowly, expecting to see nothing...and screamed.

The thing was opaque, its innards visible beneath a revolting layer of pale flesh that was covered in mucous. It had a thick, segmented body with short limbs that ended in three fingers with long, curved claws the color of old ivory. It had no visible eyes, but rather a circular opening in the center of its face that apparently served as nose and mouth all in one.

The only sound it made was a dense, watery breathing and the swoosh of its lumbering form against the ground.

With a yelp of pure horror, I leaped away, bringing my knives up and slashing desperately at its chest. My knife slid and stuck in the gooey covering.

Grimacing, I slashed again. My second blade sliced more cleanly, but barely managed to catch skin and did little damage. The skin looked thin because of its opacity, but it was like leather beneath the slimy covering.

The thing rose suddenly, resting its copious weight on its back segment, and flailed at me with the short front limbs. I easily avoided the monster's flailing limbs, but didn't even see the real weapon coming.

A long, black tongue snapped out and slammed against my cheekbone, sending me stumbling backward on a cry of pain. Instinctively, I reached for the wound and nearly stabbed myself in the eye with my knife.

I was disoriented and dizzy from the attack, but I couldn't take my eye off the nasty bug for even a second. I lunged awkwardly forward, and stabbed at it with my knife.

The tip of my blade broke off in the thick skin and my hand slid off the hilt. I yelled as the blade sliced through my own palm, and barely managed to hold onto the weapon.

Irritation exploded through me.

"That's it!" I yelled, trying to wipe the greasy goo off my hands so I could hold onto my weapon. "Now you've ticked me off."

I danced backward, away from the creature, making its head snap up in surprise. After my screaming, it had no doubt expected a full-frontal attack. I fully intended to attack, but I needed to change my tack.

I closed my eyes, knowing I had a second, maybe two, before the monster attacked. Tension thrummed from my inability to see. Fixing my mind on what I needed to do, I tugged at the power spooled in my core. Justice and I had been practicing to grow my traveler magic and fine-tune my ability to use it. Though I'd been thrown into my role as an inter-dimensional cop, of sorts, I'd been functioning on my newly elevated ability with blades combined with sheer stubbornness. Justice and I had recently been working on improving other aspects of my new abilities. At first it had been overwhelming to discover I might have actual magic along with my ability to bounce, but I'd learned to appreciate the fact that I had backup skills which might someday become useful. Though I'd never used them outside of a training session, my instincts told me they might be the only thing that would save me in my current predicament.

So, I plucked at the thread of energy, giving it a firm tug just as a slight vibration in the environment warned me that the sluglike monster was on the move.

Fighting my instincts, I kept my eyes tightly closed and dodged sideways, my feet moving as if they rested on a current of air. I stopped mere inches from a bent pillar of rock and ducked as the monster's nasty tongue slammed out, fracturing the rocky protuberance and sending painful shards of filthy rock flying toward my face.

My inner sight flared and I swung my first blade, spinning into a dip to slice again. Both strikes hit gold and hot blood splashed over me. The creature's cries were a high-pitched keening. I sent out my inner sight and saw that it was doubled over, its attention no longer on me. But as I moved close for the killing blow, the tongue punched out again and I barely danced away in time to avoid a direct strike between my eyes. If I'd been using my regular vision, I'd have been dead. With my eyes open, Justice had taught me, my other senses interfered with my ability to truly see.

Traveler magics were attuned to the world around us in a way our other senses couldn't manage. Since we traveled to dimensions and locations where sight and hearing were often compromised, we needed to be able to rise above the use of our more limited senses.

I spun again, my blades held one above the other, my arms outstretched. It was a dance of death. A leap of violence. Another strike, and then another, and the creature fell to the ground, dead. I could hear its death in the silence of its watery breaths. The vibrations of its fall were enough to shake the rocky skeleton of the dark, nasty cavern.

I planted my feet and opened my eyes, realizing as soon as I did that my chest was heaving from my efforts. My heart was pounding. With that realization came the memory of why I was there. I slipped my blades back into their sheaths and started off in the opposite direction from the one the slug monster had been herding me. A dull yellow light permeated the space, seemingly originating from someplace high above my head and emerging from the shadowed roots of the bony projections.

The passageway widened, the rocks beneath my feet worn in a clear traffic pattern. All I heard for several minutes was the steady plop and drip of cold water, running off the tips of the bony protrusions like raindrops off a roof.

Then I heard other things. At first it was little more than buzzing in the distance. The sound was so unlike human conversation that my brain didn't take any notice of it until I'd been listening to it for several minutes.

When I finally realized what I was hearing, I jolted to a stop, ducking behind a fracture in the concrete wall and crouching down to observe the source.

I waited several minutes before movement in the shadows warned me they were coming. My pounding heart made me breathless and I forced myself to take slow, deep breaths.

Voices exploded into the passage. I jumped, my hands tightening on my weapons as a trio of figures emerged. They were dressed in rough filthy robes and carried some kind of wide bowl balanced on long sticks.

The three women were nearly white they were so pale. Their eyes were mere slits, too small in their round faces. Their sallow white cheeks were smeared with a black, greasy-looking substance and their hands looked equally filthy. They spoke in quick, unintelligible sentences and nodded their heads often, their wide, flat feet slapping heavily against the worn path.

When I realized they were probably harmless, I started to stand. But one of them spotted me before I could move.

The tiny woman with tangled blonde hair jolted to a stop and released her end of the two sticks. Her hands framed her lips and she sent a barrage of tiny, hard projectiles toward my face. I realized after a beat that she was spitting them at me, fast and hard as if from a pellet gun. The woman in the middle grunted as the extra weight of the bowl's contents fell to her. Liquid splashed from the wide bowl as the two women struggled to keep it flat.

In the meantime, the tiny woman continued to pelt me with what I realized were tiny rocks that had sharp edges.

My knives weren't going to do me much good against them. I tried holding up my hands. "I'm not going to hurt you!" I yelled, before realizing the silliness of the statement. They weren't in any danger from me, since they were the ones doing the hurting.

A tiny projectile glanced off the soft skin just beneath my eye and I yelled in frustration, shoving to my feet. "Stop it!"

All three women screamed and threw up their hands, letting go of the sticks. The bowl crashed to the ground and broke, its disgusting contents slithering out of the debris and dispersing across the floor.

With a cry, the women hit their knees and clambered after a quickly escaping mound of nasty, wormy things which reminded me too much of the slug monster for comfort.

Behind them, a husky yell went up and I decided it was

time for me to move on. I was vaguely aware of one of the women responding to the call as I leaped over a slithering mass of nastiness, jumped the tiny woman's legs, and kept running. Behind me, the women screamed again, followed by an explosion of the strange, chittering language they'd been speaking.

I needed to find someplace to hide, and fast. Heavy footsteps were heading my way. "Who is it?" a man's voice bellowed and my steps faltered. He'd spoken English. The women's chittering voices lifted to respond, the sound carrying easily through the passage.

The heavy footfalls picked up speed until they were running.

They were close. Really close. And I had to make a quick decision.

Hide or fight?

Since I had no idea how many were coming, I thought it would be wise to hide and see what I was up against first.

As a group of robed figures emerged from the shadows of the passage ahead, I dove sideways, into a crevice in the rock which was barely wide enough to accommodate my wide booty. Backing deeper into the fissure, I forced myself to take deep, slow breaths so they wouldn't hear me wheezing like an asthmatic water buffalo.

Deep, rough voices joined the women's chittering in a brief conversation. I peered outside, praying they didn't think to look for me in the hidey hole. But the three men who'd arrived just after I'd hidden simply helped the women recapture the nasty squiggly things and then barked something that had them all turning back the way they'd come and hurrying away.

My shoulders drooped as relief slid through me. Still, I kept my attention outside my hiding space in case they decided to return. That was my only excuse for not realizing that I wasn't alone in the crevice. My first clue was when I backed into something squishy and it gasped. The rock crashing against my skull was the next, and last, clue.

As well as a pretty good indication that I should have been paying better attention.

15

WE'RE GOING TO SAVE HIM

I hit the ground hard, my limbs heavy and my mind muzzy from the assault. I was vaguely aware that I needed to move...to protect myself...but my body wouldn't follow the instructions my battered brain was sending out.

Footsteps scuffed my way and a figure loomed over me, the rock still in hand. I tried to sit up and pain arched through me, making me suck in a gasp and clasp the blade on my left hip, out of sight of my attacker.

I wasn't entirely helpless if I had a weapon in my hand. Though I was just as likely to stab myself as the creature threatening me with a rock.

I tensed for battle, my fingers tightening on the hilt of the knife.

The figure above me doubled and then tripled.

Gah! I couldn't fight off three people. I could barely form a coherent thought.

The figure reduced back to one and moved closer, small pale face framed by a rough hood. Darkness obscured the attacker's features, but I read a sudden hesitancy in its stance. The hood tilted. The rock lowered a few inches.

I prepared to attack.

"Rae?"

Huh? Was I hallucinating? It couldn't be... I frowned, certain my brain was scrambled and I was hearing things. "Mols?"

"Sweet cherubs on a full moon!" she exclaimed before catching herself and slapping a small, filthy hand over her mouth. She dropped to her knees beside me. "I can't believe you're here."

I rolled to my back, groaning. I couldn't stretch my legs because the crevice wasn't wide enough, and my neck was bent against the slimy rock wall. "I can't believe you hit me in the head with a rock."

I thought I saw her grimace, but I might have been imagining it.

"Sorry! I thought you were one of those nasty squinty-eyed people." She reached down as I struggled to get off the ground and put her hands under my pits, helping me sit up. I leaned against the wall and sighed. Reaching up to touch my head, I winced at a stab of pain. "From now on, you're not allowed to play with rocks. You haven't shown responsible rock-wielding behavior."

Molly laughed. "I've missed you," she said, throwing herself at me.

Despite the pain her assault caused, I hugged her back. "I've missed you too."

I shifted and my leg landed on something squishy. It squealed and I levitated off the ground. "What!?"

Molly made a disgusted sound and stomped on the squealing critter. "It's those nasty things the mole-people eat." She gave a full-body shudder. "Disgusting."

"They eat those?" I asked, equally disgusted.

Molly nodded. "They tried to make me eat them too."

"Did they taste like chicken?"

"Ha," she said, her lips twitching. "I said they *tried* to make me. I threw them away."

"How did you get here?" I asked my friend. "I've been looking all over for you."

She sighed. "I'm not sure. One minute I was hitting one of those giant mutants on the ear with my city classic pump and then we were in some weird water place with a lot of fog."

I looked down at her tiny feet. They were mostly hidden by the robe, but I thought I could make out naked toes on one foot. "Please tell me you didn't damage the shoe? Those are my favorites of all two hundred pairs of your shoes."

She cocked a hip, glaring at me. Since I could only barely make out her expression in the low light, the attempt lost much of its power. "I did, unfortunately. The upper sole split right in half." She looked thoughtful. "It's not a total loss though, I'm going to tell the designer to put stronger soles in the design. Maybe a spike in the heel. We can call it the Commando City Classic Pump and charge twice as much for it as a combo weapon and kick-butt shoe."

I snickered. "You always were good at identifying a niche market," I told her.

Molly nodded, looking thoughtful. She frowned. "Where're Justice and Elvo?"

The reminder made my heart hurt. "I don't know where Elvo is. We had to leave him behind."

"You what?"

"Justice made me." I winced, sounding like a five-year-old trying to blame my brother because I punched him.

"You're lucky I'm down to only one shoe or I'd pound

your fool head with it. What were you thinking? That dog's the best thing that's happened to you in years."

My dignity came alive, straightened its shoulders, and glared at her. "I beg your pardon?" Like I needed a pet to feel whole. I wasn't one of those women who collected dachshunds like glass figurines.

No, my evil conscience said, *You collect shoes instead*.

"Shut up," I told my conscience.

"Rude," Molly said.

"Not you. I was yelling at the voices in my head."

She stared at me.

"What?"

"You just told yourself to shut up. I'm wondering if that rock did permanent damage."

"Well, stop wondering," I snarked back. "It did."

"How did you find me?" she asked, wisely changing the subject.

"You don't have time for that story. What's the deal with the tiny-eyed people?" I asked. "How did you end up with them?"

"I'm pretty sure those ugly whiskered guys sold me to them. They stuck me in a cell at some kind of weird market for a while and then brought me here."

"What for?" I asked. As soon as the words left my mouth, I knew they might have been a mistake. "Scratch that. I'm sure you don't know why they brought you here."

"Oh, but I do. The mole-people were going to sacrifice me to that giant mole thing." She shuddered so violently she dropped her rock. "Apparently, they make a sacrifice every three months on the full moon. And it has to be an outsider."

"Why an outsider?" I asked.

"Because they were running out of locals to sacrifice."

"Okay," I said as if that made perfect sense. "What are you doing in this crevice?"

She looked disgusted. "Isn't it obvious? I'm escaping."

"Good," I said, shoving to my feet. "Let's get out of here." I stopped, frowning. "You haven't seen Elvo?" I don't know why, but I'd assumed they'd both ended up at the same place. Yeah, I know about assuming. It appeared the truth of that old adage was hitting me between my green eyes. I ran a hand through my hair. The short, curly strands were matted down on one side and stuck straight up on the other. I must have looked delightful. Good thing I wasn't vain.

Not totally. On the plus side, my boots still looked pretty good. Despite the abuse I'd put them through. I needed to tell Molly how well they'd held up. Later. First things first.

"We have to find Elvo," I told Molly.

She nodded. "Of course we do."

"I have to take you home first."

She punched my arm.

"Ow!" I rubbed my arm. "Why the violence?"

She tried to get all up in my face but her five feet two inches just wouldn't allow it. She ended up glaring at my boobs. Poking me with a finger, she said, "Stop treating me like a helpless ninny. I'm going with you to save that poor puppy and I don't want to hear another word from you about taking me home."

I rubbed the bony part of my chest where she'd poked me. "Stop it, Mols. You're denting my boobs."

"In your dreams. I'm not touching your boobs." She got an evil glint in her eye. "Besides, if I was, that would be the most action you'd seen in years."

I punched her arm.

"Ow. WTH!"

"Violence breeds violence," I said smugly.

"Let's go," she said. "I think I might know where Elvo is."

"Where?"

"Just come with me, I'll show you."

I reluctantly followed her to the mouth of the crevice. Molly stuck her head out and looked both ways. The passage was blissfully empty. She popped out and hurried back the way I'd come.

"I ran into the mole monster down this way," I told her.

She blew a raspberry. "I'm not scared of him. I have my trusty rock."

My skull throbbed at the memory of her rock. "That thing would dispatch your rock with one snap of its nasty tongue."

She screeched to a stop and I almost ran into her. "Warn a girl," I complained. "Your brake lights aren't working."

Molly put her hands on her trim hips and glared up at me. "You saw the monster?"

"I killed it."

She punched me again.

"Ow! Jeezopete, Mols."

"Why didn't you tell me you'd killed it?"

"I don't know," I whined, rubbing both arms. "Maybe because I have a concussion and two broken arms because of beatings from my best friend."

She sighed. "Don't be a baby. Okay, that changes things. Come on."

"Where?"

She left the path and ducked beneath one of the giant stalactites, stepping around an oily puddle and shoving a strange brown plant away from her face. I hurried to catch up with her, splashed into the puddle she'd avoided, and drenched my long-suffering boots and jeans. "Slow down," I growled, my shoes squishing embarrassingly. "Where are we going?"

"This is a shortcut," she told me as she stopped and looked around. She took off again, the hem of her rough robe darkening from the filthy water that seemed to be getting more plentiful by the minute.

A horrible stench filled the air. I grimaced, covering my nose. "Ugh! What is that?"

"Monster poop." She sniffed daintily. "We're close to its den."

I looked around as a feeling of dread crept up my spine. Knowing what I was looking for, I could pick out large piles of white stuff dotting the area, which I presumed was the monster poop. "Nice scenery."

She didn't turn around, but I could almost hear her roll her eyes. She stopped and looked around again, frowning.

"Lost?"

"No. I've only been here one time. They harvest the slugs here and they made me help." Molly grimaced at the memory. "We need to go into the monster's cave."

That didn't sound good. "Do you think Elvo's in the cave?"

"Don't be silly, Rae."

"It was a fair question."

She expelled a disgusted breath. "That time I was there, I remember seeing figures etched on the walls inside. I asked about them and Watch told me they were image magic. Meant to ward off the slug monster during the times between the sacrifices."

"Watch?"

Mols nodded. "He's the one who guards the sacrifice and the camp." When I just stared at her, she added, "They're named for their tasks at the camp."

"Well, that's...practical."

Molly reached the opening of the cave and stopped, holding her palms up as if testing the air. "Do you feel that?"

I felt a prickling in the air. A stinging touch that signified magic. "You can feel it?"

Her gaze found mine and held, something unreadable in her eyes. Finally, she nodded. "I can."

"Is that..." I hesitated, not sure I wanted the answer to the question I was about to ask. "How long have you been able to feel magic?"

Her flinch was so slight I wouldn't have seen it if I hadn't been watching her closely. She shrugged. "A while."

She wasn't telling me the whole story. I wanted her to elaborate, but she turned away and stepped into the cave.

I stepped through the opening and nearly ran her over. She'd stopped just inside, her tiny form rigid as she stared at something deeper inside the cave.

I followed her line of sight and gasped. "Is it always like this?" I asked softly.

She gave me a rigid negative shake of her head. "Maybe it's because the monster's dead?"

"Maybe." I stepped around her, my mind sliding back to the information I'd learned at the Travel Bureau. What had Fair said about the levels of magic?

Red is a top three hot color. Only orange and yellow are hotter.

I stared at the orange mist in front of us. It bathed the entire main part of the cave, thickening to a bright yellow fog in front of the back wall. Dancing within the yellow mist were an array of images, crude representations that seemed more terrifying for their brutal depictions.

The monster I'd killed dominated the center of the dancing images. I recognized the deadly tongue and the nasty, segmented body. Something gushed from a wound in its side and a figure in a rough, hooded robe stood over it with a long spear. Around the pair were a menagerie of other monsters in cages, most of which appeared to be asleep. Leading away from their prostrate forms, depicted as wavy lines, their magical energy joined at the figure's head, encircling him in stolen power. My gaze caught on a particular cage, with a particular massive black dog and my heart broke. "They have him in a cage?"

Molly sighed. "He looks much worse than when I was here." She turned to me, a sad expression on her grungy face. "I don't know if we can save him, Rae."

"What are you talking about? There has to be a prison somewhere with an annoying but strangely endearing Hellhound mutt in it. We're going to find it and save him."

She shook her head. "The creatures in those cages change. The ones here, with the exception of Elvo, are different from when I was here last. They've...drained them and they died."

Swallowing hard against the horror, I shook my head. "No. He's still here. That means he's alive."

Tears slid down her cheeks. "Look at him," she urged in a broken whisper.

I looked. Despite my instant denial, I couldn't help seeing how pale the image of Elvo was. I couldn't keep from noting the paleness of his glowing red gaze. Or the emaciated aspect of his huge frame. Tears burned my eyes but I blinked them away, sniffling. "We're going to save him."

16

SUPERIOR LEADERSHIP ABILITY

Molly scraped a hand under her nose and stayed silent.

Think, Rae, I admonished myself. Stop feeling sorry and think. *There has to be a way...* My pulse spiked. I turned to Molly. "Is this a physical place? This prison?" The cage Elvo was in looked a lot like the place where we'd left Elvo. The magical market. "Have you seen cages here?"

Molly shook her head. "Not here. The only cages I've seen were in that market place. She narrowed her eyes. "What are you thinking?"

I was thinking I might be a little crazy. I started to pace, taking care not to let the orange mist touch me. If I did what I was thinking, I'd have to take Molly with me. Would she survive the trip? According to Anil, I'd made Rog sick when I'd bounced with him. I couldn't risk my best friend in the same way.

Then there was the time factor. When I left Elvo he'd been healthy. Had they had time to drain him so severely?

"Rae? Whatever you're thinking, you'd better do it fast. I hear them coming."

I shook my head. Too terrified to risk Molly in a bounce. But she could see and feel magic. Did that mean she wasn't a null like Rog? Could she survive? It didn't matter. I couldn't risk her. If something happened to her I'd never forgive myself.

I turned to Molly, grabbing her arms. "I need to go someplace for a few minutes. Can you hide from them until I get back?"

Her pretty hazel eyes narrowed. "You're not going anywhere without me."

I couldn't hold her gaze. I couldn't risk her in a bounce, but I'd learned that the dang-blasted sub dimensions didn't always bring me back to the same place. If I left her, I might not find her again.

Voices broke the silence outside the cave. They were close. Too close. I had to move.

I paced faster, torn by my options. I couldn't leave Elvo behind again. Could I? *No!* I rejected the idea as soon as I had the thought.

"This isn't your decision, Rae," Molly told me. "It's mine."

"It's too dangerous, Mols." I briefly considered telling her what had happened to Rog. But I couldn't do that to her. She'd be overcome by grief and she needed her wits about her until I got her out of there.

"You're wasting time and the mole people are almost here. Just admit I'm coming and let's do whatever we need to do."

I shook my head. "Molly, I can't..."

"You can," she said, cutting me off. "And you're going to."

A sharp command tore through the cave and I reacted,

reaching for Molly with the idea of making her hide. But something went wrong. Energy flared in my core, painful in its intensity, and I felt a bounce building beneath it.

As a stocky man with small eyes and long, tangled white hair burst into the monster's lair, a deadly spear clutched in his hands, the world was already bending. I grabbed a memory of the time and space I was aiming for and opened my mouth to scream as agony sliced through me. We slammed down hard, slicing off my scream. Hitting the ground on my knees, I skimmed forward, slamming into hard metal bars. Behind me, the sounds of snarling and snapping were accompanied by the clank of metal against metal.

Climbing slowly to my feet, I felt a hundred and ten years old. The knees of my jeans were stained with black dirt and blood from the crash landing. Blood flecked my lips. I tasted it on my tongue where I'd apparently bitten it.

Beside me, Molly groaned. I turned to her and panicked at the blood pouring from her dainty nose and running down her face. "Mols! What happened?" She yelped as I grabbed her shoulders and launched her off the floor in a panic-induced move. Lowering her feet back to the ground, I scanned her tiny form, eyeing her for green skin and bloat. "Where does it hurt?" I pressed on her stomach, envisioning internal injuries.

"Umph!" She flapped her small hands, trying to drive me away like a pesky fly. "Stop helping!" She glared at me, irritated by my fussing, but all I could see was the blood coating her pale face.

"What can I do to help you? Do you need to lie down?"

Her hands came up in a defensive maneuver. "No. Step away. I'm not going back down there and being wrenched off the ground again. You almost cracked my head against the top of the cage."

Heat flooded my face. "Sorry. Adrenaline overload. It happens a lot." I brushed gently at the dirt on her sleeve and she relaxed. I punched her on the arm.

"Ow! WTH, Rae?"

"I told you it was too dangerous for you to bounce with me. Now look what you've done."

We cast our eyes on the big black dog, thankfully looking pretty much as I'd left him, and the one remaining rat-man.

Molly slid a quick look over the rodent-like human and shuddered. "I thought the mole people were gross."

I nodded in agreement. "And they are."

A bark yanked my attention back to Elvo. He had the rat-man's head mostly in his mouth and was eyeing me with irritation as the guard tried to cut him with a strange, circular blade.

"Good dog," I said, giving him a thumb's up.

Elvo growled.

I turned my glare back to Molly. "Do you see what I was talking about? This place is dangerous."

"As opposed to the last place where I was," she snarked back.

I opened my mouth to argue, but had to concede her the point.

"Besides," my bestie went on. "So far you're the only one hurting me." She used the sleeve of her rough robe to wipe blood off her face.

Huffing out a sigh, I said, "I came to rescue *you*. How did I lose control of this op?"

"You ran up against superior leadership ability."

The rat man gave a muffled scream and something

cracked. The guard went limp and Elvo opened his enormous maw and let his victim drop to the ground.

Molly and I grinned at him. She gave a happy little squeal and hurried over, wrapping her arms around his thick, furry neck. "You're okay. I was so worried."

He tucked his head around her and sighed. Molly looked like a toy doll next to the big dog. I hurried over. "Hey, buddy. I'm glad you're okay."

He gave me another growl, but his tail swept the dirt floor once.

"Who wants to go home?" I knew it was a silly question, but the thought made me happy. Home. Finally.

Elvo's tail made a cloud of dust behind him.

Molly raised her hand. "I do." Then she frowned, and her eyes widened as panic tightened her features. "Rog!" she shrieked. "We have to help him. He tried to scare that thing off that was stalking me, but apparently a stapler isn't a very effective weapon against giant rats." Her lips curled with contempt. "Rae, I knew you were into some weird stuff, but, A. I didn't think I was going to get dragged into it too, and B. I had no idea how weird."

I blanched. "Sorry, Mols."

She shrugged. "You can explain later. We need to get home and check on Rog."

Heat flooded my face as dread filled me. I was going to have to tell Molly I might have killed her assistant whom she, inexplicably, loved like a friend. "Yeah. About that."

17

COME FOR A SWIM

"Bloated how?" Molly asked. "Like he's having a bad period, or like he's spent the last two months under water?"

I grimaced. "The latter."

Molly's legs attempted to wobble out from under her before Elvo moved in to give her something to hold onto. Her small, pale hand clutched his thick black fur and I watched her fight tears.

It was like a knife to my heart. "I think he's going to be okay, Mols. I got him help as fast as I could." I hated to risk giving her false hope on top of everything else. But I had to believe Rog would be okay. The alternative was just not acceptable. "Come on," I offered her my hand. "I'll take you to him."

The quiet prison cave was gradually becoming less quiet. Distant voices rose above the sound of the pig things squealing and I knew we'd run out of time. Whatever had run them off before was apparently no longer a problem.

My gaze slid to the dead guards. It was only a matter of time before they were discovered and the cage we'd voluntarily put ourselves into would become a permanent prison. I looked at Elvo. He chuffed softly, moving closer so I could bury my fingers in his fur.

I looked at Molly. "Hold on, we're going to bounce again."

Her eyes went wide. "Wait. Can't we just…"

The world hiccupped and curved around us, and I thought of Rog, hoping we'd end up in his room on Aere. But something failed in the middle of the bounce, something tore, and agony sliced through my chest, turning my vision white under the exquisite pain.

I slammed down on carpet, the sun too bright in my eyes. I was vaguely aware of Molly grunting in pain and Elvo slamming into the room behind us.

I writhed on the ground, my throat pulsing around an agony-laced scream. Jagged claws cut from steel ripped into me, tearing chunks of my flesh mercilessly away.

The sun burned into my eyes and broiled my skin, and my limbs flailed stiffly, out of my control.

Molly's alarmed voice sounded far away, her shrieks for help surreal against the pain. I clutched the rug beneath me, praying for the pain to stop. My throat was raw from screaming, and my body was exhausted. I didn't realize I'd been seizing until the convulsions finally stopped. With their cessation, some of the agony softened. I still felt as if someone was clawing out my insides, but the pain had lessoned enough for me to stop screaming.

"Rae!" Molly crouched beside me, the filthy hem of her rough robe rubbing up against my bare arm. Her hands touched my cheeks and I felt her sobs in my battered core.

I reached out blindly and found her hand. Her small fingers wrapped tightly around mine and her breath bathed my face. "Rae. Talk to me. What's wrong?"

What was wrong? I sighed and even that small amount of air was like blades scraping over my tonsils. I swallowed, wincing. "Water?"

She moved and I pictured her nodding. "I'll get it. Stay there."

I think I wheezed out a laugh, There was no danger of my moving.

Too much, my mind scolded. I'd bounced too many times. Carrying Molly twice and Elvo once on top of my earlier bounces had overloaded my system. I was paying the price for that. I was only glad Justice wasn't there to scold me. I'd be fine with some rest and...

"Here," Molly said. "Sit up and open your eyes so you can see the glass."

Sitting was a mistake. All the pain that had been shooting through my insides collected in my belly and pulsed there, each throb of pain doing a great job of imitating jagged glass. I had to hold my breath for a beat, waiting for the wave of pain to pass, before I could drink.

Elvo lay down next to me and gave a soft whine as I settled back against a chair. "It's okay," I assured him, though I wasn't at all sure it was. The last time I'd overdone the bouncing, I'd nearly died. And, while it was true I was more experienced than I'd been then, with a bit of resistance built up, I knew the symptoms I was experiencing weren't a good sign.

I looked around and realized I hadn't managed to take us to Aere after all. I'd been aiming for the Bureau and had slammed us down in my living room instead.

All things considered, it could have been worse.

"Drink," Molly said. "I'll go get you some aspirin."

I didn't think aspirin would help, but I didn't argue. It probably wouldn't hurt. What I really needed was some sleep. Even as I had the thought, I felt my eyes drooping shut. I leaned against the chair and Elvo's warm bulk and felt my mind drift away.

"I knew you'd come," said a voice I'd never heard before but somehow recognized. "We have much to discuss."

I blinked against the wavering blue haze in front of me, the figure walking my way seemingly behind a shimmering mist. *"Who are you?"* I asked, squinting to bring the other person into better view.

The figure swayed toward me, her blonde curls floating around her shoulders as if in a magical wind. She had porcelain skin that shimmered with blue light and her slanted eyes were framed with lashes that sparked in the light from above.

I frowned. The light itself was strange, appearing fractured as it played over the white sand beneath her feet. Feet that were bare beneath the silvery wash of her gown. Like her hair, the dress swayed around her. It was cinched with a belt of seashells and tied around her neck in a rope of tiny pearls. As she stopped a few feet away, I realized a string of the same pearls was wound around her head several times like a crown. Her eyes were aqua blue and wide, the outside corners tipped exotically upward. She smiled at me and my stomach twisted with alarm.

"Traveler Kitt, we meet again."

I shook my head, the queen of denial. "You can't be..."

She cocked her head and for a flash, her lithe form was overlaid with another. One much more terrifying than the smiling woman standing before me. *"Can I not?"*

The Nessile.

"You're in your human form?" It was a stupid question but I was having trouble wrapping my mind around the reality of what I was seeing.

"*I am. You are one of very few who have seen it.*"

I frowned. "Why me?"

"*Why indeed.*" Her terrifying smile widened, the small teeth sharp enough to rip flesh. Even in her human form, she had teeth like a predator and all I could think about was what those teeth had done to Rog. "*I have need of assistance and you seem to be the one who can best help me.*"

I shook my head. "I don't know why you'd think that. I'm just a traveler."

"*A traveler with a special skill. One which few possess. You are a tracker and a warrior. You could not be more perfect for my needs if I had created you myself.*"

I opened my mouth to argue but stopped as a school of orange and pink fish swam past between us. My mouth slammed shut and my frown deepened. Had I taken drugs? The scene before me felt like a psychedelic experience. I grinned. "This is a dream," I assured her. "A really weird one."

She laughed with me, bolstering my assumption that I was having a fever-induced dream.

Then something changed.

Her teeth clacked together and she clapped her hands. The water...because that's what I realized it was... roiled violently, nearly knocking me off my feet. I clamped onto the first thing I saw, which happened to be a coral bed. The multi-hued coral sliced my skin but I held on anyway, because letting go would have seen me blown away from the Nessile, and into the black terror of the deep water beyond.

The Nessile was suddenly there, her aqua eyes flashing with rage. She leaned over me, the sound of the churning water nearly drowning out her voice as she said, "You will find the creature who stole my child and you will bring him to me."

I held very still, my gaze locked on those teeth. I wanted to tell her I couldn't bring anything to her. She was a water monster and I was basically human. Finally, I said. "Who stole your child?"

Her eyes flashed. She threw back her head and screamed. I'd thought the water was violent before, but it exploded into an underwater tornado that erupted from the sand bottom and climbed to the surface, my hands were ripped from the coral bed and I entered the spout, spinning violently while being pummeled by biting sand and small, terrified fish.

I gasped and gurgled as the water I'd so far managed to survive threatened to kill me after all.

As dreams went, it sucked pretty bad.

The spout ended as quickly as it began. The water around me slowly stilled. Though it took a moment for the debris swirling within it to settle back down to the sand.

The Nessile appeared again, her blue eyes stormy and hard. *"You will find the man who took my child and bring him to me."*

I nodded. All I wanted at that point was to get out of there. "What can you tell me about him?"

She stepped back, calming. *"You have seen him. You will bring him to me."*

I frowned. "I have?"

She turned away. *"You have three days. If you do not bring him to me, you will die. Your friends will die. The one with eyes like the ocean will die."*

"Wait, I can't come back here. I can't breathe under water."

She tapped her neck just beneath her ear and smiled. *"Can you not?"*

Pain slashed my jaw in the spot she'd indicated. I

reached up but felt nothing. The haze around me thickened again. Her form in the distance grew faint. "Wait!"

My chest ached. My head pounded. And my throat... My throat was agony.

~

"THERE YOU ARE," Molly said. Her voice held a smile as I swam back to consciousness. If I didn't know her so well, I might have missed the worry throbbing through it. My bestie's warm hand squeezed my arm and yanked me fully back to reality. I came up off the bed on a violent cough, water shooting from my mouth as I doubled over in violent spasms.

Molly yelped and jumped back, then ran out of the room and came back with a towel. "Rae, girl, what happened to you?" She frowned, reaching out to touch the spot beneath my ear. "When did you get this ink done?"

Beside me, Elvo whined, his big head dropping onto my thigh as the coughing spasms calmed. I buried a shaky hand in his fur and held on, feeling instantly soothed.

Molly sat down next to me, her arm wrapping around my waist. "Hey. You were having a bad dream. Were you dreaming about that perm you got in middle school again?"

I snorted and a residual stream of water shot out of my nose.

"Ew," Molly said, handing me the towel. "What's with the water?"

I wiped my face and sopped up the water on the bed. "That wasn't just a dream." My voice sounded husky, torn and ragged.

"What was it, then?" Molly asked.

I shook my head, dropping back to my pillow. "How long was I out?"

She glanced at the digital clock on my dresser. "Four hours. Do you feel any better?"

I swallowed hard. The Nessile had said I had three days to find her child. Since I had no idea who I was looking for, or where, that wasn't nearly enough time.

Shoving the covers back, I tried to get out of bed. Elvo dropped a massive paw on my knee and Molly blocked my way, arms crossed and a belligerent look on her face. "What do you think you're doing?"

"I have to get up."

"No. You have to rest. You look like a marionette wearing yesterday's strings."

"I can't rest. I picked up an assignment," I argued.

"I don't care, Rae. Look at you. You can barely sit up. How are you supposed to work?"

I grabbed her hand. "Can you make coffee and eggs or something? I'll have a shower and eat and I'll be fine."

She frowned.

"I promise, if I don't feel up to it after that, I'll go back to bed." I hated to lie to my best friend, but I had no choice.

Finally, she expelled a frustrated sigh. "Promise?"

I held up my pinkie finger and she curved her delicate pinkie around mine. "Pinkie swear." We held each other's gazes for a beat, then she grinned. We'd been pinkie swearing since kindergarten, when we'd bonded over badly drawn pictures of our families and learned to have each other's backs on the playground, which had been the equivalent of a prison yard at school, complete with bullies, cliques, and wardens.

When she'd left the room, I turned to Elvo. "Here's the deal..." I quickly filled him in on the Nessile's demand and threat. Though the dog had proven over and over again that he understood me, I would have given anything at that moment for him to be able to respond verbally. Instead, I had to settle for a whine when I explained about the Nessile's missing child, and a growl when I told him about her threat to kill my friends.

"If you can contact Justice, do it now. I'm going to get ready to leave."

He chuffed and jumped down off the bed, heading out of the room. Watching his oversized furry butt pad away, I realized he was just as likely to be heading out to steal some of the bacon I could smell cooking, than to be doing as I asked.

Heaving my own sigh, I stood, winced at the pains shooting through my legs and up my spine, and then hobbled toward the shower.

18

MONSTER ALERT!

I was trying to decide between my burgundy leather ankle boots with the low heel, and my knee-high black suede flat-heeled boots when Molly started screaming.

I dropped the boot I was holding and limped into the kitchen. "What? Did you see a cockroach?" Full disclosure, I'd been battling the nasty things for a couple of weeks and hadn't been able to beat them back. I was going to have to break down and hire an exterminator.

Molly was holding a frying pan in one hand and a TV clicker in the other. She turned a pale visage to me, eyes much too wide, and pointed to the small television in the corner of my counter.

Another woman, equally wild-eyed, with hair sticking straight up from having just run a hand through it, was holding a microphone and wincing as the world exploded into chaos behind her. "Monsters!" the woman exclaimed, jumping as a roar burst into the bedlam behind her. "They're everywhere. I feel like I'm living in a nightmare."

"How'd they get here?" Mols asked me. She set the hot pan back on the stove and turned to me. "Rae, what's going on? First they invaded The Muddle, and now this."

I recognized the buildings behind the reporter. She was standing in the square, a busy spot for restaurants and shopping in the center of town. I rubbed my hands over my eyes and looked again. Nope. Still there. "They must have used the portal..." My words trailed off as I considered that. Justice and I had shut the portal down. And, yes, a couple of the rat things had escaped with us. But we'd killed them.

"Woof!" Elvo spun toward the living room, tail wagging.

I didn't even have time to ask him what he was barking about before Justice and Juggler appeared.

"Whoa!" Molly exclaimed, jumping back. "That's going to take some getting used to."

Before I considered what I was doing, I'd hurtled myself into Justice's arms. He caught me, barely, with a look of surprise. "You're okay," I murmured into his warm throat.

He patted my back stiffly, clearly uncomfortable with the PDA. "I am. But we have a problem."

Embarrassed, I stepped away from him and pointed to the television. "We saw."

"What happened?" Molly asked. "Why are they here?"

"That's a good question," Juggler responded. He didn't get a chance to say anything else. A small form stepped out from behind him. I jumped as Molly squealed just behind me, nearly barreling me over in her attempt to get to Rog.

She wrapped herself around him with another squeal. "I can't believe it's you. Rae told me how she nearly killed you."

"Hey!" I objected.

A suspicious cough had me turning a glare on Justice. "Shut it, you."

He laughed. "You did kind of do a number on him, Rae."

I shrugged. "It wasn't on purpose. Besides, the Nessile did most of the damage." The reminder had me frowning. I didn't have time for whatever was shaking out in the city. I needed to find the magical reptile's offspring and bring her abductor to the sea monster before she made good on her threat to hurt everyone I cared about.

Rog fixed me with slightly bulgy brown eyes. I stiffened, waiting for the onslaught. The man and I had a rocky relationship to start with. My nearly getting him killed via Nessile and over-bouncing wasn't going to improve it. I opened my mouth to head him off with an apology, but forgot to speak when he said. "I know where he is."

I frowned. "He who?"

"The man who took her kid. I can see where he is."

I felt my eyes go wide. Did Rog have magic after all? More importantly, how did he know about that? "Who told you...?"

Juggler shook his head. "I can see what you're thinking, but no. He's still a null. He's just saturated with magic at the moment, and it's strengthened his tether to the Nessile."

My gaze flew to Rog. "You're inside her head?"

"No. Nothing like that. I'm just seeing...visions...I guess is the right word. I saw the kid. And I saw him take her."

"That's good," I said, smiling. "That's really good. Tell me where they are."

Rog cocked a brow, planting his hands on his hips. "Why would I do that, *Kitten*?"

I growled. "Because it's a matter of life or death, *assistant*."

He glowered at me. "You're a total screw up. You brought those things here and got Molly taken, nearly got me killed, and now the whole city is overrun with monsters. How did you manage that? The last thing I want is to be tethered... whatever that means...to that monster. I just want to find a bottle of gin and a pizza and bury my feelings in them."

Molly saw me stiffen and shook her head. "There's no time for you two to feud. Like Rog said, there are monsters in the city and we need to stop them."

The room erupted as everyone realized she was including herself in the mix. Even Elvo whined, bumping her thigh with his massive head.

Molly held up a hand and glared at the dog, rubbing her thigh. "We're wasting time. I'm helping. What can I do?"

"That's really the question, isn't it, Mols," I said, trying to remain calm. "What can you do against a city full of magical monsters?"

She mirrored Rog's hands on hips glare. "Watch yourself, Rae. I'm not letting you guys go out there and risk yourselves while I stay here safe, so you'd better give me something to do."

Justice groaned. "I'm getting an unfortunate sense of déjà vu."

"Me too," I said, glowering at Rog. I cranked my brain for a minute and then glanced at Justice. "Ideas?"

He sighed. "Guns. That's all we've got for her." He narrowed his eyes when she perked up. "But you're not to shoot non-monsters."

Molly saluted happily. "Sir, yes sir!"

Justice looked to me for clarification. I shrugged. "It's a soldier thing."

He nodded. "Let's go."

"I'll drive." I knew better than to try bouncing again so soon. My mama didn't raise no fool. Maybe an idiot. But not a fool.

We'd made it to the door when a shrill whistle stopped us.

I spun on my heel to find Rog striding toward us with a meat cleaver in his hand.

"Oh no!" I said. "You're still recovering." Besides, he had to survive so he could tell me where the Nessile's brat and her abductor were. My friends lives depended on it. My kid's life…I shook my head. If I even thought about my daughter being in danger, I wouldn't be able to function.

"I'm coming," Rog insisted. He twisted his wrist and a tassel on a throw pillow fell to the ground. I blinked. I'd barely seen him move.

Rog grinned. "It won't last long, I'm sure. But while I have it, I intend to use it."

Justice and I shared a look and he gave me a miniscule nod. He was right. We'd need all the help we could find.

Even if that help was next to useless in a fight and wouldn't recognize desk assembly instructions if they climbed up his left nostril.

Yeah. I went there.

"You can go," I told him. "But if you get in the way or get hurt, I'm knocking you out until the battle is over."

Rog's hand moved, a blur of motion, and an auburn curl drifted to the carpet. "You can try."

THE DOWNTOWN square area of Fort Wallace, Indiana had been built around City Hall, a picturesque structure created from sparkly white stone blocks and surrounded by well-kept gardens. The area was the heart of Fort Wallace, and featured a large grassy area overlooking the river. I'd spent many an hour sprawled over that grass, enjoying marginally famous bands and local artists performing live theater under the stars.

Being the second largest city in Indiana, Fort Wallace could sometimes draw a band whose best times were behind them but who were still fairly popular. But we rarely got entertainers who were at the top of their game. Still, we had a beautiful fine arts building, regional historical museums, and a semi-pro baseball team that actually did pretty well in their league.

The downtown square featured a ton of small, quaint shops as well as restaurants running the gamut of coney dogs, an Indiana favorite, all the way up to expensive steak and seafood restaurants. I wouldn't say we were on par with the larger cities across the country, but we had less crime and the size was perfect for me.

We found a place to park not too far from City Hall, and set off on foot, tension thrumming the air between us.

"Stop swinging that thing around," I scolded an over-exuberant Molly. "You're gonna hurt somebody with it." I shoved her gun hand down so the muzzle pointed harmlessly toward the street.

Next to her, Juggler waggled his brows. "I can't stop swinging mine. It has a mind of its own," he joked. "But I can promise I won't hurt anyone with it. I'm all about pleasure. Not pain." His brows danced as Molly snorted.

I drew a knife and pointed it below his waist. "If that thing swings anywhere near Molly or anybody else around me, it's going to be decorating the asphalt. Got it?"

He winced in mock terror. "Got it." But he gave Molly one last waggle of his dark brows before nodding toward a distant cluster of people standing in the middle of the street. "I'll go check that out."

We watched him jog away and headed on down the street. Despite the news report, the center of the city seemed fairly quiet at the moment. I could hear raised voices and a couple of car horns in the distance, but nothing all that different from the normal sounds of downtown Fort Wallace.

"Maybe they moved out to the fringes," Molly said, sounding disappointed.

We turned a corner and chaos hit us in the face.

At first my brain couldn't wrap around what I was seeing. There had to be five or more monsters running rampant on the streets. Cars lay on their sides, doors torn off and windows smashed. A news van was upside down on the asphalt, its bumper resting on the sidewalk and all four wheels spinning. A torn body lay in the gutter, his life blood draining into the sewer grate and one hand outstretched toward what had probably been an expensive camera.

"It looks as if the news people aren't going to have images to go with their reports," Justice murmured into my ear.

I frowned.

A woman screamed and my gaze whipped that way. I spotted the reporter who'd been on the news only minutes earlier. She appeared to be running for her life. Behind her was the bear we'd run from at the market. The reporter had kicked off her shoes, or lost them in the chaos, and was doing a fair job of staying ahead of the bear. But it was only a matter of time before the creature caught her.

Justice and I shared a look and he nodded. I touched his hand and looked at Molly. "Protect that woman. Get her into a building and barricade the door. Use that gun only on monsters," I warned.

She nodded, her hazel gaze dark and huge. "I will. I promise."

I spared a second to give her a quick hug and then we bounced. The bear must have sensed our bounce, it was ready for us when we landed, a massive claw swiping through the air toward Justice. He easily danced aside and slashed one of his trademark, fanlike blades over the bear's middle. It bellowed and reared up onto its back legs, baring its belly to Justice's other blade.

I took a running start and leaped onto its back, one arm going around its thick, furred throat and the other jamming my blade into its back. Its roar grew louder, more enraged. The creature spun, trying to shake me off as I continued to attack.

Meanwhile, Justice had scored several more slashes on the creature. It was nowhere near dying, the thing was apparently built of steel, but the blood loss was beginning to slow it down.

I dug my feet into its fleshy hide and strengthened my grip, "I'm going to try for its throat," I yelled at Justice.

He started to nod, but his eyes went wide and he yelled, "Watch...!"

The world twisted sideways and slammed down. The shock of the bounce caught me off guard and I lost my grip with all but one hand. The creature wasted no time rearing up again and, before I realized what was happening, its deadly claw had found me.

It scraped along my arm and I yelled, losing my grip and hitting the ground on my back. The impact knocked the wind out of me. I lay there for a beat, wheezing. The bear monster dropped down to four feet and lumbered slowly toward me, its enormous maw opening on a bellow, lips vibrating under its immense power.

I felt the bellow in my chest and was scrabbling backward as fast as I could move. I could have bounced. Should have bounced, but seeing that monstrous bear lumbering toward me at full speed, I panicked. I only had time to grab my two blades and lift them, before the massive bear leaped off the ground, and crashed into me.

19

YOU'RE WELCOME

The gunshot got lost in the snarling sounds of the bear. As I tried to wrap my mind around the fact that the creature wasn't ripping me to pieces, Elvo slammed into it, driving its limp body off me. Shoving slowly to my feet, I looked up and blinked at the small figure running my way.

Molly.

Adrenaline still surging through me, I rounded on her. "I told you to stay inside and protect the reporter. It's not safe for you out here."

Molly's jaw tightened and her slender dark brows lowered. "You're welcome."

The snarling sounds behind me ramped up a few notches and I turned to find Elvo jerking his big head and ripping a large, furry chunk out of the bear. The monster gave one last twitch and then went completely still.

Elvo chuffed as if to say, "So there!" and turned to trot back our way, licking his chops.

I grimaced. He stopped next to me and rested his head

on my arm, looking up at me and whining. I patted his soft head. "I'm okay. Thanks for the assist."

He chuffed.

"What about me?" Molly asked, pointing the gun at the bear and feigning a shot. I was relieved to see she knew enough not to put her finger on the trigger.

Then it hit me. "You shot the bear?"

She nodded proudly.

"Mols, he was on top of me. We were like one target. Do you know how easily you could have missed him and shot me?" My brain was imagining all the ways that could have gone horribly wrong.

"I know. It was a really good shot, right?"

I closed my eyes, horror sliding through me. "I've imagined dying in many ways over the years. Never did I think I'd go down from friendly fire by my best friend."

She laughed.

Laughed.

"Rae, we've known each other for what...five decades give or take? Do you really not remember my short but intense love affair with Hank the shooting range manager?" She waggled her brows in a way that reminded me all too painfully of Juggler. "Hank taught me many fun and useful things."

I made a gagging motion. "TMI, Mols." A distant scream tore me out of the moment. "I need to get back to work. And you need to get back to that reporter."

She shook her head. "She called for a ride. A news van picked her up a few minutes ago and tore out of the city. A guy was filming from the back as they sped away."

"Jeezopete in spandex," I sighed. "There goes any chance of containing this."

Molly gave me a smug grin. "I wouldn't worry about it.

Before they left, I removed the battery from his camera."

I stared at her, astounded. "Who are you and what have you done with my friend the fashion queen?"

She grinned. "Honey, fashion is a multi-faceted business. In my early days I did everything. Design, cleaning, documenting. I know cameras like I know the back of my hand."

"I still want you to stay close to me."

She nodded. "Happily." She stared after Elvo's quickly departing furry black butt. "It looks like I'm all you have."

I grimaced at the two big rats down the street. They were fighting over the dead carcass of an enormous yellow snake. Elvo headed for the rats, his eyes glowing a fierce red. It took him no time at all to grab first one and then the other, shaking them hard enough to break their necks.

"Rae!"

Justice's deep voice sounded slightly panicked. I scoured the area, looking for him. A moment later, Elvo shot full speed toward an alley about a block down the street. He disappeared into the shadows.

I took off running, vaguely aware of Molly's small feet pounding along behind me. A Chickara, an eight-foot-tall bird monster with no feathers except for the red, white, and black spikes on top of its flat head, gave a death squawk and fell over in front of me, its sword-like beak clacking together an inch from my leg as I jumped the head and kept on running. Juggler stumbled out from behind the massive bird monster, covered in green, stinky blood.

Behind me, Molly complained loudly about his stench and I smiled. I'd been covered with Chickara blood, which smelled like rotten fish, once before. It hadn't been fun.

At the mouth of the alley, I skidded to a halt and pressed against the warm brick wall of a pretty flower shop. Even with the shop shut up tight, I could smell the sweet scent of flowers until Juggler showed up and poisoned the air with his stench.

"What's going on?" Pressed against the wall of a bakery that sold the best donuts in the city, Juggler peered around the corner and frowned. "I heard Justice yell, but I don't see anything in there."

He was right. I'd expected to find my partner flailing beneath a pile of monsters, fighting for his life, but the alley appeared empty.

Or...maybe not.

As I slipped around the corner, moving past two rusted dumpsters that smelled even worse than Juggler, I noticed a soft green glow ahead. The illumination rode the air above a crumpled form. As I moved closer, the single glow broke into two, and then split a few more times.

"What is that?" Molly asked, coming up next to me.

I didn't have any idea.

A voice addressed us from the street. "Aere spirits."

We all turned to Rog in surprise. Elvo stood next to him and the small man had one hand curled into the Hell-hound's scruff.

"Um, what?" Molly replied.

He joined us in the alley. "I saw them when I was getting healed. They..." He frowned. "They're made up of magical residue."

"Are they friendly?" I asked, feeling silly for the question as soon as I asked it. The unmoving body on the alley floor beneath them was a pretty good indication the glowing things weren't helpful spirits.

"Not in my experience."

Molly gaped at her non-magic assistant.

Seeing her look, Rog shrugged. "They pumped me full of magic trying to heal me from the Nessile bite. There was a lot of residual magic in my room. I woke up one night and saw them. I called for help and that woman...what was her name? Fair?...came in and extinguished them with some kind of spray. She told me they were foul spirits and that she'd gotten rid of them. She also said I had nothing to worry about." He frowned. "I don't think she was telling me the truth. I never did quite shake the feeling that they were still there." He eyed the glow at the end of the alley. "I don't suppose anybody has some of that spray?"

I sighed. "That would be too easy."

Juggler tossed his strange, circular blade from hand to hand and winked. "Let's see what these things are made of."

We watched him stalk toward the glowing energy balls hanging in the air. When he got within a few feet of them, he stopped, eyeing the unmoving form on the ground. "It's Justice."

I was striding forward, knives in my hands, before I'd made a conscious decision to move.

"Rae..." Molly started to say.

I cut her off with a curt, "Stay back. Both of you."

Elvo's enormous form trotted up next to me, his body a warm wall against my thigh.

I was five feet away from Justice's unmoving body when the residual energy struck. The biggest one shot toward my face like a rabid hummingbird and I barely managed to duck in time to avoid it. It took me a beat to realize I hadn't avoided it. Not totally.

Elvo yowled in pain, a thin line of blood showing against his heaving sides where the hair had been removed with surgical precision.

My pain was like fire against my scalp, it brought me to my knees, my entire body shaking under the force of it. Someone screamed and I straightened, turning. "Molly!"

She and Rog were lying on the gritty alley floor, their arms over their heads.

"Molly!" Panic filled my voice when she didn't respond.

A pale hand finally lifted and waved. "We're okay. The thing didn't want us..." Her words cut off with another yelp and she pressed herself into the ground as the ball of spitting blue energy shot past again, a few inches over their heads.

Heading directly for me.

"Jeezopete in knickers!" I screamed as it flew toward my face. At the last second, I did a limbo maneuver and the thing missed me by inches. I slashed at it with my knife and, amazingly, found my target with the wild swing.

My moment of elation was short lived. It was like sticking a fork into an electrical outlet. Wild electrical current danced over my blade and slashed into me, cutting and burning me from the inside out. I hit the ground screaming, my body twitching uncontrollably as I succumbed to an electrical energy I had no defenses against.

I couldn't even bounce to get away from it. I could only lie there, thrashing helplessly, as it ate away my insides. At some point, I begged for the oblivion of unconsciousness, just to get away from the pain.

The agony stopped.

I lay there panting, afraid to move for fear it would come back. The alley had filled with a strange haze that reminded me uncomfortably of an Aqua subD. I sat up, wondering if I was dreaming, and then remembering how real the dreams in that place were. The Nessile had nearly killed me inside a similar subD.

With that thought spurring me on, I jumped to my feet. I clutched my blades tightly in my hands, my sweaty palms making it harder to hold onto them. My gaze slipped over the natural shadows of the alleyway, their murkiness even deeper than normal. But I saw nothing.

No rabid residual energy. No friends. No partners. The alley was empty.

A small figure appeared twenty feet away. The delicate features were vaguely familiar. The old-fashioned dress, too frilly for current fashion, and the long blonde curls tweaked a memory I couldn't quite grasp. The little girl appeared to be about ten years old.

She stopped a few feet away and gave me a smile, her turquoise gaze sparkling with good humor. The memory clicked into place. "You're the girl from the market. The one who told me to hide in the crevice."

Her smile widened. *I am.*

I blinked as her voice played inside my head. Her lips hadn't moved. Thinking back to that first time we'd met, I realized they hadn't moved before either. "Why are you here? Are you responsible for those energy things?"

The quick negative shake of her head sent glossy curls dancing around her slender arms. *I only wished to use this moment of unconsciousness to give you a warning.*

"About what?"

The child's smile slid away. *My mother has commanded you to find me. She attempts to force you to find my guardian and bring him to her. You must not do this.*

All the pieces fell together and my eyes closed as I realized what was happening. "This has all been an attempt to bring you back."

The little girl nodded. *I left of my own volition. My mother is needlessly cruel. For millennia, Nessile have served as a rational voice of power and control in Aqua. We have no leading bodies, no rulers, but it was necessary for someone to keep the millions of divergent creatures in line to avoid total chaos. She* frowned. *I fear that, in her reckless cruelty, Mother has tipped the delicate balance of the world and will cause it all to come crashing down.*

"She threatened all my friends and loved ones."

The child nodded. *I am aware of that. I have come to ask you not to interfere. My guardian has a plan to deal with my mother. I am an important part of that plan. If mother gets hold of him, she will kill him and we will lose our leverage.*

"What leverage?" I asked. I wondered what kind of power it would take to defeat a creature as powerful as the Nessile.

The girl shook her head. *I cannot divulge that. I am sorry for your loved ones. But I must ask that you leave them to their fates. Your destiny is sealed. You will become stronger than you should and you will be a force to be reckoned with in all worlds. I look forward to working with you soon, Traveler Kitt. But what will be, must be.*

I shook my head. "I won't let them die."

She sighed. *You must. As you have seen, my mother's reach is unstoppable. If you do not allow us to do as we must, all worlds will suffer under her chaotic and deadly rule.*

My head shook in the negative. It couldn't be true that we were helpless against the Nessile's machinations. Stopping creatures like her were the reason for the travelers' existence. There had to be some way we could fix the current problem.

Stay out of it, Traveler Kitt. This time I am asking. Soon, I will take things into my own hands. I do not wish to do that...

The child's voice faded away and the haze in the alley lightened, until only the normal darkness obscured my vision. I blinked, looking up at a bright, silver moon hanging high above the dank alley.

An unnatural silence grated against my nerves. I sat up,

groaning at the tightness of my muscles and the pain still throbbing in my scalp where the residual magic orb had zapped me. I pushed to my feet, happy to see that the nasty balls were gone.

Then my gaze slid downward. To the unmoving bodies of my friends and partners strewn over the cold ground. "No!" I screamed. I ran to Molly, finding her pretty hazel eyes open and already glazing in death.

Rog wasn't breathing.

I let loose a feral scream, beyond control of my emotions. I turned and ran to Juggler. Like the others, he wore a death stare, his usually jaunty smile turned to a grimace.

And sprawled next to him...

Elvo!

I collapsed beside them. A sob escaped and I turned to face the final blow. Justice hadn't moved since we'd entered the alley. I was afraid to approach him, knowing what I would find. His handsome face was tight in death, locked in the contortion of agony, the black marks all over his body telling me what had happened in his last moments.

I dropped to my knees and wailed, a scream of loss throbbing in my throat as I threw my head back and gave in to my insurmountable grief.

It couldn't be.

It wasn't possible.

It wasn't real.

They couldn't all be gone.

But only *my* screams broke the silence of that death-riddled alley.

And only *my* lungs rose and fell with life-sustaining air.

They were all dead.

20

CRAZY CAT LADY?

S omeone was shaking me. I swatted at the insistent grip, unwilling to climb out of oblivion and face the loss of all my friends.

But the grip was unrelenting, and the voice that accompanied it even more so. "Rae! You've got to wake up," the voice insisted.

I swatted in the direction of the voice, needing to be left alone. But it spurred something inside me. Some memory... some realization.

"What's wrong with her?" another voice asked.

"I don't know. Maybe those things charred her brain."

A rough, wet caress bathed my arm and the memory coalesced into realization. *Elvo?* Had the death of my friends just been a brutal dream? My eyes shot open and I looked into the wide, black face of a Hellhound. I was too stunned to avoid the wet stroke of a stinky dog tongue, wetting a path from my chin to my eyebrows. "Ugh! Dog breath." Tears burned my eyes as I wrapped my arms around the big dog's neck. He smelled like fresh air and ozone, with a tinge of alley stink staining the edges. "You're alive."

"We're alive too," said a snotty voice. "If you care."

I narrowed my gaze on Rog.

"I told you she liked that dog more than us," the assistant told Molly.

My bestie was grinning. "That's okay. She hasn't dated in a while. I guess we can just be relieved she hasn't stocked her house with a hundred cats by now."

I laughed before I could stop myself. "You know I can hear you, right?"

"So can I," said a deep, sexy voice.

I looked up at Justice, who stood grinning down at me. "I thought you were dead," I told him, my voice quivering.

His frown told me he might have thought so too...for a time. "Those things have quite a bite," he agreed. "But they don't seem to be fatal. Just really painful."

"Where did you go?" Juggler asked, his tone thoughtful.

"Huh?" I said, dazzling him with my wit. "What do you mean?"

He cocked his head. "That was more than just being unconscious," he said, still thoughtful. "Or even a dream. You had a vision, didn't you?"

I didn't want to talk about how horrifying it had been to see them all dead. I never wanted to think about it again. I suspected the girl had been proving a point to me. Foreshadowing what she would do if I didn't stop looking for her and her abductor.

But that vision had probably scarred me for life.

Shaking my head, I forced a smile. "Those energy things kicked my butt." I held a hand up to Justice and he tugged me off the ground. I stumbled forward under the strength of his assist and hit his chest. My gaze found his and a quick surge of interest made my stomach flutter. Placing a hand over his hard, warm chest, I held his intense stare for a moment. His heart beat strong and sure beneath my palm. Relieved, I stepped away. Something snapped between us, like a rubber band breaking, and I felt off balance for several minutes as we started back to the car.

I looked around as we came out of the alley. Broken glass glittered beneath street lights and the overturned vehicles were still there, twisted and dripping fluids. But there were no bodies. "Where are the monsters?"

"The Bureau sent cleaners to take care of them. The human victims who lived are having their minds cleansed of the episode and the ones who died have been positioned in plausible situations for their specific wounds and forms of death."

I stared at him for a beat, my mind shattering over the size and complexity of that task. "They did all this in a few hours?"

Justice dropped an arm companionably around my shoulders. "They were very motivated."

We turned down the street where I'd parked my car. "What about the news channels? The report we saw before we came down here. And that reporter was filming when we arrived."

Justice shook his head. "The reporter will be convinced she saw a bunch of escaped zoo animals instead of monsters. A correction will be going out soon on all the channels. We took care of the cameras, disabling the ones that were left behind as well as the ones that were driving away as we arrived."

"How?" I hadn't meant for my voice to sound so irritated, but I thought they were all taking the issue much too lightly.

"We have people on the ground in Terro for just this kind of cleanup. As soon as word went out that we had a monster problem, those people were dispatched."

I frowned at Justice. "But how?"

"The news crew probably didn't notice the powerful magnet in the back of the pickup truck that pulled up next to them at the light," Juggler said, grinning.

I reached my car and opened the driver's side door. But I didn't climb inside. I shook my head. "Guys, there were probably dozens of people on the street and in those buildings who saw what happened. What about them?"

Juggler and Justice shared a look.

Icy fear climbed down my spine. "What did you do to those people?"

When nobody spoke for a minute, Rog said, "It was really cool."

I turned a glare on him, and he smiled wider. "It was. They called her a siren, but she didn't lure anybody onto rocky shores. She sang away their memories, that's all."

I looked at Justice and he nodded. "Nobody was hurt. They all just fell asleep and, when they wake up in the morning, they won't remember what happened."

They seemed to have an answer for everything. With a sigh, I climbed into the car and waited while everyone else piled inside. "How is it you weren't caught up in the siren's song?" I asked Molly. She was in the back seat, sitting between Juggler and Rog.

Mols held up what looked like lumps of seaweed. "The siren gave us ear plugs. They worked like a charm."

I was really starting to feel like I'd been left out. I would have liked to have met the legendary Siren.

Justice tried to close the door but Elvo leaped in before he could. The big dog draped himself over his unhappy partner, his butt pressed against the door and his big paws on the console between the seats. As Justice groaned under the dog's weight, and the back seat whined about the doggy smell, I started the car and pulled away from the curb. A giant head on my shoulder, weighing me down.

I drove slowly through the downtown streets, a bit spooked by the unnatural quiet of the area. There were no cars on the street, no people walking along the sidewalks. "I just can't believe nobody will remember that happened." I'd spoken softly, to myself, and didn't expect anyone to hear me, given the lively conversation in the back seat. But Justice turned to me and nodded. "This isn't the first time this has happened," he said. "The Bureau has gotten really good at fixing things."

"And there are never leaks?"

He thought about that for a beat and then said, "Occasionally the creature known on Terro as Big Foot is spotted when he gets careless. Also, Nessile occasionally like to show themselves just to get a reaction."

"The Loch Ness Monster," I murmured.

He nodded, his gaze searching. "Tell me what happened back there."

I stiffened, my hands tightening on the steering wheel. "Nothing happened."

"Rae..."

I held up a hand and gave him a look that I hoped would stop him from pursuing the subject. I eventually needed to tell him what had happened in my vision with the little girl. As my partner, he deserved to know. But I had no intention of talking about it in front of the others. "I'll tell you later," I said softly.

He watched me a minute longer and then gave me a slow nod.

"Drop me back at The Muddle, please," Molly said from the back. "I need to start clean-up and secure the place."

I caught her grimace in the rear-view mirror.

"My customers are probably wondering why we've been closed."

"You can't go back there, Mols," I said, my tone gentle. "It's too dangerous."

She shot me a mulish look. "I'm going. If you drop me at home, I'll just take myself there."

"I'm going too," Rog said.

"Suck up," I murmured.

"I'll go with them," Juggler offered, surprising me.

Elvo barked hot, dog breath into my face. I frowned at the dog. "Et Tu, Brute?"

He woofed happily, his fringe of a tail smacking Justice in the face.

I scanned Justice a look. He nodded. "If they get into trouble, Juggler can bounce them out of there."

Sighing, I nodded. "Okay. But if you get yourselves killed, I'm going to hurt you."

Molly snorted. "If I die, I'm going to haunt you forever," she threatened. "It's going to be epic."

"Good luck with that," I said, my lips twitching. "I'll get you exorcised and salt the place to keep you out."

"We'll see," she said, a smile in her voice.

JUSTICE and I did a quick perimeter check of The Muddle, finding the neighborhood about as quiet as you'd expect for that time of night...or really morning. We scoped out the area where the portal had spit us out after our near-death experience on the rat-infested ship, finding no sign that the rat things, or anything else had recently come through.

Juggler and Elvo checked the interior of the store and reported that it was secure.

I stood in front of the building, warring with dual needs. I felt guilty leaving Mols with the mess the monsters had created. It might have been illogical, but I couldn't help thinking I'd caused the monsters to be there. They'd come because I'd botched the portal closing.

"It's not your fault," Justice said, startling me. I'd been so buried in my thoughts, I'd forgotten he was there.

I shook my head, tears burning my eyes. I blinked them back and shook my head. "The portal…"

"Was there long before we came through," he said, interrupting. "You didn't bring it here."

I glanced at him. He looked weary. I'd never seen him look less than vigorous and strong. Seeing him with fine lines framing his sapphire eyes was more disturbing than it should have been. He ran his hands through his unruly mass of light brown hair, pushing the sun-kissed strands away from an unlined forehead. "Okay, I think we've earned a rest," I said. "Two hours of sleep and then I have to leave. I have something I need to do."

And I had no idea how to do it.

He didn't respond until we were back in the car. Then he turned in his seat and fixed me with an unrelenting stare. I barely kept from flinching. "What?"

"Tell me."

I stalled by starting the car and clipping on my seat belt before pulling out of the lot.

"Rae," he warned.

I chewed my lip. I really didn't want to tell him about the girl because I knew he'd want to come with me. Or worse, he'd try to talk me out of it. After that horrible vision of all my friends dead, I didn't want any of them to join me on my quest. "It's a personal matter."

He crossed muscular arms over his chest. "Tell me."

I glared at him. "Keep your nose out of it."

"You promised you'd tell me what happened to you in the alley."

An uncomfortable silence pulsed between us. When he didn't relent, I finally sighed. "What happened to me back there...it wasn't the first time I've been dragged into a vision."

He frowned but didn't comment, so I went on.

"The Nessile yanked me into one beneath the water. I could breathe there. But the most interesting thing was that she was in human form."

I sensed his interest and gave him a smile. "I didn't see that one coming."

He gave me a reluctant grin. "I'd heard rumors, but didn't know for sure they could do that."

Nodding, I went on. "She wanted me to find the man who'd taken her child."

He shifted in his seat. "Why you?"

"She claimed I was the perfect one to do it. I think because I'd been a cop." I shook my head. "I told her I couldn't do it and she told me she'd kill everyone I cared about if I didn't."

I let silence fall between us for a moment as Justice took that in.

Finally, he said, "So, the Nessile visited you again in the alley?"

"No." I stopped the car in front of my apartment and killed the engine, turning in my seat. "Her daughter did."

His eyes widened slightly. "You found the kid?"

"She found *me*. Strangely, the little tyke doesn't want to go back to mommy dearest."

Justice snorted. "I saw that movie. It's a good analogy."

"Thanks." I smiled. "Anyway, the kid told me they were

working on a plan to overthrow the Nessile because she was cruel and chaotic."

He nodded. "I'd heard something along those lines. To tell you the truth, I suspected the rats in the sinking ship were her handiwork. It suits her peculiar sense of humor."

"You think she set this whole thing up to draw us in?" That was what I thought, but I wanted to know if it was a crazy idea.

"It's highly possible."

I deflated, nodding. That meant what happened to Molly and Rog *was* my fault. Even if indirectly.

Justice was staring at me again. He had a questioning look in his eyes. I knew what he wanted to know, but I couldn't tell him that. I'd rather die than go through the memory of that horrible dream again.

I opened my door. "Let's go inside. I need to get some rest and figure out what to do next."

21

DEATH WILL BE YOUR FRIEND

"You don't have to do this," I told Justice two hours later. "This isn't your problem. It's mine."

"We're a team," he said, looking irritated with me. "That makes it *our* problem. Besides, you're not going to be able to get away with this by yourself. You need an abductor."

I frowned. "I don't like it." I'd laid out my plan to stop the Nessile, but Justice had pointed out the single fault in my scheme. And as much as I didn't want to admit it, I did need his help. "What if she strikes as soon as you show up?"

"She won't." He sounded so sure. I wished I shared his certainty.

"You don't know that."

"The Nessile is a vain and arrogant creature. Striking me down too quickly will rob her of the chance to gloat and savor her victory."

I suspected he was right.

"Besides," Justice continued. "We only need to keep her distracted long enough for the girl to arrive. Then, hopefully, she'll be too busy to worry about us."

I'd shared with him my gut feeling that the Nessile's offspring would step in if she thought her mother was in real trouble. The kid seemed determined to stop her mother's despotic rule, but she didn't seem interested in taking out her parental unit by deadly force. "*If* she arrives," I agreed, not feeling all that certain about my gut when it put Justice at risk of being hurt or killed. "But I'm not as confident in my plan as you seem to be." I scrubbed my hands over my face. "This is a desperation play, Justice."

His smile made my stomach flutter. "And you've never pulled one of those off before?"

I shrugged. I had, actually. Probably more often than not. As a cop, my gut had always been a pretty phenomenal asset. "Yes, but I've never done it when the stakes have been this big."

He stood and placed a warm hand on my shoulder.

I looked up into his incredible eyes and felt myself turn to mush. Hard on the heels of the wave of pure lust, came the vision in my head of him lying motionless on the ground. Dead.

I shuddered violently.

He pulled me into a hug and I tried to resist. I knew better than to give in to his nearly irresistible pull. But he held me there, his deep voice rumbling against my ear, along with the strong beat of his heart. "You are the smartest woman I know," he said, his voice deep and sure. "Your technique isn't always perfect..."

"Hey!" I objected.

He ignored me. "But your instincts are generally right on. You've got this."

I sighed, allowing myself to lean into him for just a beat. "Are you sure about the spell?"

He hesitated just long enough for me to pull away and look into his eyes.

"Justice?"

"I'm sure. I've used it before. I trust Juggler."

Apparently, Juggler was not only both a guide and a traveler—an unusual feat in itself—but he was also something of a spell-builder. "Please tell me his spells work better than his pickup lines." Juggler had successfully used the Travel Bureau's step retracing spell, but that didn't mean he could create effective spells of his own.

Justice barked out a laugh. "Only marginally." When I tensed, he added, "But we only need it to work for a few minutes, right?"

"I don't..."

He stopped me in the only way that was guaranteed to shut me up and make me forget what I was saying. He kissed me. It was a sweet kiss. A tender brush of lips that was warm and exquisitely soft. It demanded nothing, only offering comfort and affection, but it left me puffing like a beached fish. When he broke the kiss, I backed away, my hands coming up as if to ward off another kiss. "That's not..."

"Shall we go?" His sapphire eyes sparkled with amusement at my panicked reaction. "Time's wasting."

I briefly considered having it out with him about the kiss. But, if I was honest with myself, I hadn't exactly pushed him away. And his jovial manner implied it hadn't meant any more to him than a way to offer comfort. I nodded, reaching for his hand. His skin felt hot and smooth against my palm, but when I looked up into his eyes, they were no longer blue.

They were a deep, chocolate brown.

Interestingly though, the irreverent sparkle was still there.

The world around us bent and unfurled, leaving us standing on the dock with the ugly shack that had taken us to the underground market.

In the distance, a succession of glistening humps rose and fell above a charcoal gray ocean that boiled and churned. The sky above us was leaden, the air heavy with latent rain.

"She looks peeved," I told Justice. He nodded and the movement drew my attention fully back to him. He was a couple of inches shorter than his real form. The molten brown gaze intense as it looked upon what, from our vantage point, appeared to be a truly hostile sea monster. The form he wore was as close to my memory of the man I'd seen only once as we could get. The muscular frame, longish dark brown hair, and full, sculpted lips could be off a titch. I could have mixed some of the man's features with Justice's, who also had a perfect mouth and a long, straight, aristocratic nose. But the hope was that the Nessile would be too distracted by my showing up that she wouldn't look too closely.

I leaned closer to Justice, caught off guard by the foreign aroma of clean sweat and rich soil that were all I could remember of the man's scent. My quick perception that he'd just come from a forest where he'd been digging or planting hadn't even been one I'd acknowledged until Justice had put me through a memory exercise that had given us the basis for the spell, and the end result standing before me.

Unfortunately, I didn't know the man's name. I prayed she didn't ask me to give her that.

"Any ideas how to get past the tortoise?" I asked softly.

Justice...or the abductor...cocked a brow and produced a

peach he'd held hidden in one closed fist. The fruit was harder than it should have been, clearly not fully ripened. I doubted the enormous turtle would mind.

"Hello," I said to the tortoise. I held out the peach. "I come bearing gifts."

The creature eyed me thoughtfully for a beat. I got the impression it was trying to decide if I was worthy to pass.

I set the peach down on the dock and backed toward Justice. My twanging nerves aside, I forged ahead. "I've been on a quest for the Nessile." I nodded toward Justice, whose hands were loosely bound in front of him with rope. "I have brought her what she requested."

Very slowly, as if it perfectly understood what I'd said, the tortoise turned its leathery head toward Justice. Its mouth opened and words slashed across my mind. *Death will be your companion. Failure will be your constant friend.*

Okay, that didn't sound good. "I'm sorry?"

The creature's head snapped out and the peach disappeared. Then the enormous beast turned and ambled slowly toward the edge of the dock, gliding off the sun-bleached wood and disappearing into the water without a splash.

Slimy brown scum danced over the surface of the water, obscuring the tortoise and anything else living beneath the angry surface. A distant splashing brought my head up and I searched the chaotic horizon for the telltale form of the Nessile.

She'd disappeared from sight.

There was a wet splat behind me. I caught a large shadow in my peripheral vision and a few drops of water hit my face. I whipped around, expecting to find the Nessile floating near the dock, but she wasn't there. In fact, there was *nothing* there.

Justice was gone!

My blades were in my hands before I realized I'd moved. I crouched, my gaze scouring the surface of the water, looking for any sign of the Nessile's presence.

Even as I focused on the search, my heart raced and nausea twisted in my gut as I considered the very strong possibility that Justice would die. If he was under the water...

I wanted to scream. To howl. I was helpless. Useless. Everyone I loved was going to die because I couldn't do what the sea monster had demanded.

No! I gave myself a mental slap. If I was going to have a chance of saving Justice and killing the monster, I needed to stop second-guessing myself.

I needed to believe I could win. Or I would fail.

With terror making my heart thud painfully in my chest, I closed my eyes and focused on a short, controlled bounce.

My feet eased into sand. Liquid lapped against my arms. Twin pains stabbed either side of my throat. The water encompassing me was more serene than that on the surface, but it was far from calm. I became aware of a constant stinging around my ankles. Like a hundred red ants biting my flesh. Opening my eyes, I looked down to see what was biting me. A dozen small water spouts had erupted from the sand, scouring everything in their path.

An enormous school of pale fish flashed past, their eyes bulging. A fishy hunter, huge and mottled brown, with too many razor-sharp teeth crammed into its wide mouth, followed the fleeing school. The sleek predator looked to be thirty feet long and likely weighed several hundred pounds.

I pressed more deeply into the large bed of kelp I'd remembered from my first vision-visit with the Nessile, my pulse pounding for fear the monstrous fish would spot me.

Peering into the blackness of the deep water above my head, I wondered why the place where I stood wasn't dark too. The sand sparkled with a silvery light.

Eying the area around me, I noted the enormous coral shelf in the distance. The surface of the coral was smooth, as if it had been worn down over a decade or more. I could picture the Nessile reclining there in her sea monster form. That might explain the illumination. If she considered the area her throne room, she would make sure it was magicked to suit her.

Directly across from me, a sunken anchor caught my eye. It was as tall as a man and its crown was only partially buried in sand, the flukes poking up at an angle. At first, I thought it was tangled in seaweed. But it wasn't all algae.

With a jolt, I realized what I was seeing.

It was Justice, bound to the anchor with thick, ropy strands of seaweed. His chin was on his chest and his golden-brown hair floated around his face. Other than the motion of his hair, he wasn't moving.

The spell was broken. He looked like himself again.

Well, dang.

I let out a small scream, swallowing a mouthful of salt-saturated water, and choked, coughing violently. "Justice!" I called, my frantic scream causing me to choke again. I launched myself off the bottom of the sand and swam in his direction, heart pounding so hard I feared I might pass out.

Tiny, silvery fish darted away as I cut across their path. A large shadow passed overhead but I ignored it. Justice looked blue, but I wasn't sure if it was because of the water or...

No. I wouldn't think about that.

I cupped his face in my hands and looked at him. His eyes were closed and his chest wasn't rising and falling.

Without thinking, I placed my lips on his and blew. As I gave him air, I used my blades to cut him free.

Come on, come on, come on, I chanted in my mind.

After what felt like several minutes, Justice's large frame twitched. A beat later, he sucked air in a violent gasp. If my lips hadn't been compressed to his, he'd have drowned again. Flailing violently, he tried to push me away. He was disoriented, looking panicked. He clearly didn't know where he was.

Covering his mouth with my hand, I wrapped myself around him and spoke into his ear. "Calm down. It's me. You're underwater. You have to breathe with me."

After a tense moment, he nodded, expelling a few bubbles as his lips met mine.

I see you've found my surprise, said a hated female voice in my head.

I whipped around to find the Nessile draped over her coral throne. "Let him go. This is between me and you."

Her laughter was musical. *I thought bringing him here was the entire purpose of our discussions.*

Something in the way she said it told me she hadn't been in the least fooled by Juggler's spell. Even before it had broken.

"I brought him as you asked. You never said you were going to kill him." I knew I sounded naïve, but that was okay. She could think me an idiot if it meant saving Justice.

She gave me a penetrating gaze with her ocean-colored eyes. I noted they were less blue at the moment and more a stormy gray. If I'd had any doubt that the roiling ocean had been her doing, I no longer did. *Your lover will die, Traveler Kitt. Your friends will die.* She gave me an evil smile. *Your daughter...*

With a growl, I launched myself at her, my blades out

and already flashing through the water as several sharks with sword-like snouts shot toward me from all directions. I hung in the water, my blades flashing as I slashed one predator after another, carving hunks out of their slick gray flesh as they tried to attack.

I thought of Justice and faltered, barely avoiding a deadly bite from a particularly nasty shark. "Bounce to Aere!" I yelled in my partner's direction, praying he'd listen to me. Guides were generally unable to bounce unless it was to return to the Travel Bureau to seek medical aid for themselves or another.

I was pretty sure the current situation would count.

As the last shark spun away from my knives, the water thick with their blood and a little bit of mine, another foe found me.

The octopus wasn't monster-sized. But, like the tortoise, it was big enough to kill me if I wasn't careful.

I bounced away, looking for a moment to catch my breath and come up with a plan. I risked a quick glance toward the spot where Justice had been and was relieved to find him gone.

Then my torturous brain suggested he might have been eaten and my relief died a horrible death.

The seconds lost in my thoughts nearly did me in. The octopus had snuck up on me, and silent as the grave, it had wrapped its tentacles around the kelp bed I was hiding inside. The powerful appendages tightened like a noose, creating painful pressure around my chest.

I struggled to cut myself loose, but the creature only tightened its grip, making it impossible for me to breathe.

Sweet cherubs on a crescent moon. Couldn't a girl have a minute to think?

22

KELP ME RHONDA…KELP, KELP ME RHONDA

I thrashed in the octopus's deadly grip, trying to bend my wrists in impossible ways to slice the thing with my blades. I didn't hope to cut myself loose, but if I surprised it with pain, maybe it would loosen its grip and I could slip free.

No such luck.

The best I could do was to avoid the creature's nasty teeth and hope to tire it out. If it was like octopi on Terro, it could inject poisonous toxins into me from its mouth, which was on the underside of its body. A haze of cloudy substance floated away from the creature and I assumed that was its toxin. Hopefully contact through the water couldn't poison me.

It's a pity really, the Nessile said from her royal perch. *You could have been a useful ally.*

I had only one option and it wasn't going to be easy. Still, I'd been training for it, and there was just the teensiest chance I could make it work.

But first, distraction. "Your daughter doesn't want you to

find her," I said, closing my eyes and trying to find the thread of magic nestled in its hidey hole within me.

Your lies will not deter me, Traveler.

"It's not a lie," I responded, searching frantically for the elusive thread. "She understands that you're not well. You have a sickness of the mind. She only wishes to stop you from hurting others."

There! A micro-thin, gossamer thread flared bright gold in the depths of my mind. I did as Justice had taught me and fought the urge to grab for it. I needed to be very still and relax my mind so it would come to me.

Yeah. Relax. While fighting an octopus that was trying to kill me and carrying on a conversation with a crazy... woman? fish? monster?

Piece of fish cake.

The water roiled and churned. A dozen water spouts, bigger than before, erupted into existence around me.

The octopus didn't seem to notice, which cemented the notion in my mind that she was controlling it somehow.

Your lies will get you killed, the Nessile threatened.

I took several deep breaths and let my inner vision soften, visualizing my magical core opening like the petals of a flower.

Nothing happened.

It was nearly impossible to grab onto my chi when fighting for my life.

The octopus gripped me tighter and we surged free of the kelp bed, tearing the root—the hold fast—free of the rock it had been gripping.

Despite losing my only shield from the octopus, I closed my eyes and went very still, defying my situation in a desperate bid to ease my raging thoughts.

The thread eased free of my mind's grip. Not a lot, just enough for me to carefully grasp...

The sand beneath my feet erupted violently and something long and beefy shot upward, blasting into us.

The octopus released me and tried to swim away, only to be swallowed whole by something I could only call a worm. The creature was massive and probably hailed from prehistoric days.

I reacted without thinking, darting too close to the coral throne and its nasty inhabitant in my attempt to avoid the worm.

Without warning, a long, muscular tail ensnared me, lifting me higher in the churning water. The Nessile gazed up at me, a toothy grin on her leonine face. Looking at her huge form stretched out on the coral throne, I realized she looked just like a dragon, except for the fact that she had no feet. Only gem-encrusted fins.

Out of the frying pan and into the fire, the sea monster queen said with a grin in her voice.

With nothing earth-shattering to add to that, I decided to go back and try to grab my inner voice again. Not surprising, the thread was gone.

I wanted to cry.

The water behind the Nessile swirled and I blinked as Justice appeared. He had some kind of bubble around his head and his signature fan-like blades clutched in his hands. Our gazes met and locked. Warmth blossomed in my chest and he winked.

I laughed.

And the Nessile started to turn.

Her attention divided, she loosened her grip on me just enough that I got a blade free. I wasted no time slashing a long, deep cut in the meaty appendage holding me aloft.

The monster's gaze whipped back to me and the tail tightened, holding me in a death grip.

I couldn't breathe, couldn't retaliate, My bones creaked from the pressure and I knew they'd start breaking in seconds.

As I stabbed madly at the Nessile's tail, Justice half climbed, half swam up onto the coral throne. His large form dancing in the water, he swung his blades like a ninja, cutting deep grooves in the sea monsters long body. His attack tore her attention from me and she turned to him with a pain and rage-filled roar.

The tail that had me in its grip retracted and then flung outward, sending me spinning through the water in an out-of-control tumble.

A passing creature snapped at me, missing my shoulder by inches. A school of brightly-colored fish darted apart to make room for my thrashing form.

I opened my arms and spread my legs in an attempt to enlarge my profile. My frantic hope was that I could snag onto something before I'd traveled so far away I'd be lost inside the deadly aquatic world. By the time I slammed up against a sharp-edged bed of coral that looked like a burst of orange flowers, my guess was that I'd traveled a quarter mile. I could see the water churning in the distance where Justice fought the Nessile, but I couldn't make out many details.

I needed to get back there.

I needed to use the magic I hadn't mastered yet to help Justice.

I needed to work fast.

Fighting the urge to bounce back and leap into battle, I closed my eyes. I struggled to ignore the pain of a hundred small wounds and bruises along my back and shoulders. The thread glowed and pulsed deep within my mind, waiting for me to take it up.

I reached for it with spectral fingers. Grabbing hold, I gently tugged.

Nothing happened.

The thread still danced just beyond my reach. I tried again and again with the same result. I was about to give up and bounce back to Justice when it hit me. I was trying to wrap the inner sight magic into a physical construct to attack the Nessile. When I'd battled the mole monster with my inner sight, I'd been successful because I'd eschewed the physical senses, and used a much more powerful and elusive sense.

I'd fought with the metaphysical, rather than the physical. What I needed was not a physical entity. I couldn't defeat the Nessile using a physical mindset. Physically, she was much too powerful for me to subdue. But metaphysically...

With a sudden knowledge of what I needed to do, I opened my eyes and looked at the churning water in the distance. With a thought, I sent a blast of light and power surging in that direction. The enormous sea monster in the distance went rigid as the wave rolled over her.

With a second thought, I was standing next to Justice. I looked him over. He was battered and bloody, with several bite wounds on his arms and legs. I touched one. "You've been poisoned."

He gently shrugged off my hand. "It's okay. I took an antidote before I came back." He grinned. "Anil sends his greetings."

I snorted. "Right back at him." Our gazes met and

locked. I fell into the sapphire heat of his eyes, momentarily forgetting the enormous baddie thrashing against the invisible bonds of my magic mere feet away.

Blinking the spell away, I jerked my head toward the Nessile. "Shall we finish this?"

"Okay," he said, understatement apparently one of his better things. "I see you've finally overcome the mind block against your inner sight."

I nodded, grinning. "Pretty spectacular, huh?"

"Not bad. For a beginner."

I was too pleased with myself to let him annoy me. "You're just jealous."

We turned to the Nessile, weapons lifted. I saw the moment she realized she was going to die. I savored it with a bloodthirsty feeling I hadn't known I possessed.

"You were going to kill all my friends," I told her. "You threatened my daughter." I strode toward the thrashing monster, hands tightening on my blades. "You mistreated the creatures of Aqua."

Justice strode alongside me, his big form taut with barely suppressed violence.

"You ran your child off with your wickedness."

The Nessile stopped thrashing and went very still, her gaze bright with malice.

"You will die for your transgressions," I finished, my blades steady before me.

I suppressed a shiver as an icy wave of water slid over us.

The Nessile's eyes widened, but not with fear of us. Her gaze slipped past Justice and me, finding something more terrifying than we were in the black water behind us.

Awareness prickled between my shoulder blades. The icy water slowed my limbs and sent my spidey senses into overdrive.

I felt the shifting of our fates in my ice-encrusted spine. Something deadly sat at my back. Something decidedly hostile.

"Rae," Justice said softly.

I followed the line of his sight and saw movement in the shadows. Slowly, methodically, the black water split apart and a dozen terrifying creatures swam into the light.

They were creatures from another time. Creatures with eyes so small I realized they probably rarely left the shadowed nethermost regions of Aqua, the deepest parts of the largest oceans.

They were black from snout to tail. Their sleek, midnight skin was marred and pocked as if from millennia of battling for life and dominance.

Their teeth were abundant and terrifying, inspiring images of shredded and torn flesh. Massive fins, like wings, lifted away from their bulging bodies, making them look like giant, ugly birds. I guessed those fins would easily propel them out of the water if they ever ventured topside. I doubted they did, so it made sense the wing-like fins served the more practical purpose of making them motor-boat fast.

I'd heard stories about the ancient leviathan. Myths. I'd enjoyed the stories. But I hadn't believed them for a minute.

Understanding rocked my world. They were real.

The creatures ringed us, their malevolent presence a threat...a promise...of our upcoming deaths.

"What's going on?" I asked Justice.

He gave a single, brief jerk of his head, his brittle blue gaze and taut frame telling me that, whatever they were there for, we weren't going to be able to defeat them.

The herd split apart and, for a moment, I thought I was hallucinating as a pure white creature slipped into the center of the ring of monsters. It looked like the other creatures, except that it had snow-white skin and pale pink eyes that were filled with such malevolence I shuddered before I could stop myself.

It was also carrying a rider.

The little girl looked no bigger than a child's toy doll astride the enormous creature. Her long blonde hair danced lazily in the water around her, and her blue eyes seemed too large for her pale face. She was dressed in a pretty pink dress that, oddly, matched the nearly colorless pink of her ride's eyes. Her tiny feet were bare.

She glanced at the Nessile and something like sadness slipped across her delicate features. Then she looked at me, focused on my blades, and frowned.

That frown was like a physical blow. The water around us began to churn faster and harder than before. The underwater tornadoes from before returned, but they were the size of pillars on a queen's castle.

Sand rose from the bottom of the sea and whipped against our exposed flesh like sandpaper, grinding against our skin.

I struggled to keep the Nessile under my control. I briefly considered releasing her so she could deal with her daughter and her pets. But I had no idea what unleashing the Nessile would accomplish. With my luck, mother and daughter...and leviathan...would all turn on Justice and me.

With the mercurial nature of a child, the girl gave up her frown a beat later and the tornadoes receded. She pouted prettily. "We had a deal, Traveler. You went behind my back and threatened my mother."

I could have argued that I'd made no deals with her. But I didn't think she'd believe it. Her ego wouldn't allow her to imagine that I'd reject her demands. So, I decided simple and honest was best. "Yes."

If she was surprised by my honesty, she didn't show it. "Why?"

"You asked me not to give your father to her. I am honoring that request. But she has threatened my family...my friends...and I cannot let that threat stand."

The child considered my words for a beat. Her pout disappeared. "I understand. You can leave my mother to me. I will deal with her."

Yes, Traveler, the Nessile purred in my mind. *You may leave us to handle this on our own. Your involvement here is no longer required.*

I didn't like the smugness of her tone. It was clear she believed she could handle her daughter. Knowing I was going to regret it, I shook my head. "No. You won't do what is necessary," I told the child. "You'll let her live and my loved ones will be in danger."

Sand and water spouts shot into the black water high above us. The sand was so thick in the water it was suffocating and, though I tried to narrow my eyes to slits, I ended up having to close them entirely to keep from being blinded.

The water around us shifted and I acted on instinct, reaching to touch Justice and bouncing us back to the kelp bed I'd hidden inside before. The bed lay on the outer edges of a kelp forest that was as beautiful as it was terrifying. Predators lived in that forest. Multitudes of ravenous hunters that would view us as little more than their next meal.

Still, as the girl screamed an order to her sleek black monsters, I realized the forest was a better option than open water. At least there we'd have a little cover. It would be easier for us to hide our relatively small forms than it would be for the whale-sized creatures flooding our way to hide theirs.

"Come on," I told Justice.

Thankfully, he followed without argument. Because the first of the sleek black monsters was only ten feet away when we dove into the forest.

23

A BIT UNPREDICTABLE

We ran as fast as the water allowed. Which wasn't nearly fast enough. The best chance we had, since we couldn't outrun the monsters, was to keep changing direction within the kelp forest. Our heads on a swivel, Justice and I slammed through the waving, brown vegetation, dodging finned predators both resident and foreign, as well as the occasional hunk of ship debris. In fact, I would have impaled myself on a broken mast if Justice hadn't thrown himself into me and knocked me to the ground. Wrapping himself around me, he rolled us beneath the soggy, broken skeleton of the ship's hull just as a dark form glided past, thick fin-wings skimming the surrounding kelp beds.

I watched in horror and awe as the enormous fish swam slowly through the forest, its massive fins barely shifting the tall plants as it passed.

As big as they were, the prehistoric creatures moved through the forest like magic.

A second leviathan swam overhead, casting the space where we hid in shadow. We lay very still, Justice pressing me to the ground while we waited for the creature to move past. As the trailing edge of its tail fin slowly disappeared into the kelp, we allowed ourselves to relax.

A fatal mistake.

Something struck my thigh. Hard. Like a punch. I screamed before I could stop myself, and looked down at the dark blood oozing into the water.

Seeing the fist-sized hole in my leg opened the pain floodgates. I bit back a scream as agony sliced through me. Quick as a snake, a thick, bulbous head exploded from the kelp, mouth open to expose a scary amount of dentation. The dark brown fish had cloudy white eyes with large pale spots above them that looked like another set of eyes. Clutching my bleeding leg, I reacted too slowly to save myself from a second strike.

I flinched when the fish lashed out again, expecting a fresh wave of pain. Instead, Justice's blades flashed and the fish's ugly head floated to the sand, bumping against my foot as it settled.

I jerked away and then sucked in a gasp as pain lacerated my bleeding leg. I took in water with my gasp and found myself violently choking, each convulsion of my body tearing fresh pain along my thigh.

Justice dropped his bloody blade and reached for my leg.

I jerked away from his touch.

He glowered. "Let me tend it."

"No. It's fine."

The ridiculousness of that statement made him lift his brows.

I sighed. "I just need something to wrap around it to stop the bleeding."

He tore a sleeve off his shirt and held it up, yanking it away when I grabbed for it. "Let me bind it."

Exasperated, I sat back, leaning on my hands, and forced myself to hold still as he tied the sleeve tightly around the wound.

My partner kept throwing me worried glances. I kept my lips pressed tightly together and fought dizziness. The loss of blood was making me light-headed.

I'd like to say we stayed safely tucked beneath the ship's broken hull until the leviathan the sea brat had sicced on us lost interest and drifted away. Unfortunately, within seconds, the deeper problem with my wound was made real to us.

The first shark flashed past too close, its dead black eyes icing my spine. It looked exactly like what it was...a premium predator following a blood trail to its next meal.

Justice pulled me deeper under the hull and wrapped his arms around me as I shivered from shock and blood loss. My teeth clacked together as my body turned to ice. Justice leaned close, his magical air bubble pressing warmly against my cheek. "Can you bounce?" I shook my head. I'd instinctively tried to bounce us when I'd first been attacked, and nothing had happened.

He did a pretty good job of hiding his tension. But it showed in the rigidity of his grip on me. A second and third shark had arrived, their sleek gray and white bodies gliding in a tight circle around the broken hull. It was only a matter of time before one of them found a way inside.

We needed to move. But I didn't think I could run or swim. It was all I could do to stay upright against Justice. I looked into his sapphire gaze. "Can you take us to the Travel Bureau?"

"No. Keeping this breathing device active is sapping my strength."

A thunderous concussion shook the saturated wood above our heads. Sand and other debris sifted down on us and Justice tugged me closer. He was gripping me so hard I could barely breathe. I opened my mouth to ask him to loosen his grip when the sharks suddenly darted away. A beat later the hull shuddered violently under another strike.

It was a strike from something much bigger than the sharks.

The leviathan had found us.

Another blow broke the hull and it crashed down around us, forcing us onto our bellies in the sand. Stretched out on top of me, Justice looked deep into my eyes. "It's been an honor, Traveler Kitt."

My stomach twisted with the emotions warming his gaze. I reached up and placed a bloody hand on his cheek. "It's been a gas," I said, smiling through tears.

Without warning, he lowered his forehead to mine, the air bubble a spongy barrier between us. "It has been a gas." Electricity surged into me, giving me a jolt of energy even as Justice sagged. His bubble popped away and he touched his lips to mine, his skin hot despite the chilly water.

I shook my head, realizing what he'd done. "No! Justice, no."

He gave me a gentle smile. He couldn't speak without the bubble, but his gaze said it all. *Bounce, Rae. Leave me.*

I shook my head, barely biting back a sob. "I'm not leaving you." I placed my lips against his and forced them open, pushing air into his lungs.

The hull shook again and cracked down the center, dropping away from us. Suddenly, we were fully exposed to the circle of leviathan the princess brat had sicced on us. They started forward together, their small eyes locked on us.

I clutched Justice's hand and we got to our feet, going back-to-back.

Knives out, I prepared to fight for our lives. Against my back, Justice tensed to do the same.

But the leviathan stopped approaching.

Behind them, a dark-haired man emerged from the kelp forest. He walked out as if he were simply walking down a city street. Except that his dark hair floated around his head.

I recognized the strong features, and the muscular form.

He strode to a spot between the enormous beasts and stopped, hands clasped before him. He gave me what he probably hoped was a harmless smile. His eyes were brown, nearly black, and his mahogany-colored hair fell over his forehead in charming spikes. He inclined his head. "Traveler Kitt. It's an honor to meet you."

"You're the father."

He inclined his head again. "Guilty." His smile widened, gained sincerity. "I do apologize that you've been dragged into this." He frowned. "Nessie can be a bit unpredictable."

I couldn't help it, I laughed. "A bit? Yeah. Maybe a bit. Why *was* I dragged in?"

He sighed. "Nessie is a collector of things. Sometimes those things are people. She heard about the new traveler who had special skills. A traveler whose natural magic had been augmented by the stolen abilities of her maker. A traveler whose background already made her a special catch. Once she knew you existed, she was determined to have you as a useful toy."

He shook his head, opening his hands and extending them, palms up. "I attempted to talk her out of it, but she insisted you would be hers." He frowned. "I'm afraid Nessie isn't used to being denied."

"People aren't toys," I said, enraged by the devastation the sea monster had created for a stupid, selfish reason. "She hurt my friends."

"I know, and I'm sorry. When I heard what she planned, I threatened to leave her. Since she considers me one of her toys, I believed that might give her pause."

I frowned. "My understanding was that she killed her human lovers."

"Ah." He chuckled. "But I am not human."

"I take it your threats didn't work?"

"It did not. She tried to imprison me. But my friends..." He jerked his head toward the waiting beasts. "...helped me escape. When the child came with me as well, Nessie was enraged. She threw Aqua into turmoil, her destruction unfocused and widespread."

"The child came to you willingly?" I shook my head. "The Nessile told me you abducted her."

He laughed. "In her mind, it likely seemed that way. She would say I lured the child to me. But it isn't true. Little Nel knows her mother is half mad with the power. She realizes she will need to stop her. Aqua's only hope is for Nessie to be unseated."

"Explain to me how this works. I thought there were no rulers on Agua."

"Formally, there are not. However, there is an honorary role for the strongest and wisest among us. It aids in world-wide decisions and gives us an ambassador who can repre-sent us with the leaders of other worlds. For millennia, the Nessile have been our ambassadors. They are strong and considered wiser than most in Aqua, but they tend to be mercurial and sometimes don't handle the perceived power well."

"You need to take her down," I said. "Or we'll have to do it. She's threatening the people of Terro, some of which are my family and friends."

He gave me a slight bow. "You have my word. Little Nel is working on that at this very moment."

I frowned. "Are you sure she's up to it? She just sicced these beasts on us when we tried to kill her mother."

"She is torn by her emotions, but I know the child as I know myself. She will do what is needed."

I turned to ask Justice what he thought. He wasn't there. With a jolt of horror, I realized I hadn't felt him against me for a couple of moments. I swung around with a cry and saw him lying on the sand, unmoving, his gorgeous blue eyes wide.

The vision of his death in the alley rose up to terrorize me.

"No!" I dropped to my knees beside him, panic making it hard to breathe. "No, no, no, no." I shook him gently. "You need to live," I demanded.

A shimmering silver tail floated above Justice.

I grabbed my weapons and surged to my feet, facing off with the man who was a future Nessile's father. He smiled and I took a step backward, flummoxed by his impossible beauty.

"May I?" he asked, nodding toward Justice.

I rushed forward, my blade at his throat before he could blink. The water warmed and shifted as I felt the beasts moving to protect their friend.

He held up a hand and they stopped. "I can save him."

I shook my head, not trusting him. "You're a merman." I

hadn't even known they were real. But in a dimension filled with water it made sense they existed.

"I am. I can help him if you'll let me. Please let me do this. We've caused you harm. I would like to provide you with reparations."

I looked down on Justice's lifeless form and my chest broke. Agony tore a hole in my heart.

He was gone. I'd lost him. There was really nothing the merman could do to harm him anymore. But maybe he wasn't lying. Maybe he could actually help.

I nodded and the merman smiled. "Excellent." He floated to the sand, his fins holding him in place as he bent at the waist and placed two fingers on either side of Justice's jawline, just below his ears. Silver light flashed and two weird slits appeared where the mythological creature's fingers had been. The merman straightened and smiled at me. "He will breathe now."

But he didn't breathe. He might have gained what looked like gills, but he was already dead. He wasn't breathing.

In pure desperation, I dropped to my knees and placed my lips over his, pushing air into him. I reared back and did chest compressions and then breathed for him again, repeating the process for a few minutes, my heart heavy with the knowledge that I'd been too slow.

He was gone.

Pressing my forehead against Justice's, I whispered a plea. "Please live," I begged, my vision clouded by tears.

My hands clutched his shirt. I tried to shake him, hope turning to rage as I realized he was gone. All that magic and I couldn't save one, special man.

My eyes went wide with realization. *Of course, Magic*!

He'd given me the last of his magic reserves so I could bounce. Maybe I could repay the favor.

I closed my eyes and searched for the *golden* thread, seeing it pulsing within its flower-like womb inside my head. I reached for it, giving it a tug and pulling it free. The magic of my inner sight ignited. Golden light filled me, awakening heat and hope in a wash of power.

I cupped Justice's face in my palms and blew into his face. The golden energy traveled from my lips in a double thread that flowed into his nostrils. I held onto him, willing him to live.

I held my breath until I saw the first tentative changes.

A flush of color in his face.

An infinitesimal muscle twitch.

A gasp.

And finally, he jerked upright as his eyes popped open.

24

MAGICAL INK

"**I** really just thought you got new ink," Rog said as he grabbed the last biscuit from the bag.

To my great pleasure, Mols rolled her eyes at him. "Of course she wouldn't get new ink without telling me," she said, thoroughly disgusted. "Use your head, Rog." She handed me a packet of honey for my biscuit. "Gills are so unique," she said, sounding unsure. "But I think it's really hot that Justice got matching tats."

He had, in fact, gotten a permanent set of new gills from our interaction with the merman. I wasn't sure how he felt about the magical ink. I suspected he'd be thrilled with it the next time we had to do a job in Aqua. It was darned handy being able to breathe under water. On the other hand, I wondered what other magical surprises were waiting for me to discover them.

The woman who'd passed on her traveler magic to me had gotten a snoot-full of other magics from her own maker. A mix of powers that had been gained in illegal and unethical ways. She'd harmed a lot of innocent shifters in the process.

"So, everything was because the...Nessile?" Molly asked with a lift of her brows.

"Nessile," I agreed.

"This Nessile thought you and your gills would be nice to have on the payroll?"

I laughed. "Payroll no. Servitude is more like what she had in mind."

Molly said a word she rarely used, which started with a B. "All that devastation. You and Justice and Juggler nearly died. Several times. Humans died and were hurt. Rog and I suffered great discomfort."

"Hey!" Rog objected. "I almost died too. I looked like a giant St Patricks' Day sausage, remember?"

She nodded, unimpressed with the extent of his near-death experience.

"Rat men and horned bears died too," Rog added.

Molly flipped a dismissive hand. "I didn't say it was all bad."

"Plus, you and I got some magical powers out of it," her assistant said with a grin.

I slid him a shocked glance. "Wait, you don't still..."

He performed a clumsy stab at the biscuit in my hand with a butter knife. The knife tumbled from his grip and clattered onto the desk where we were eating. Rog sighed.

I grinned. "That answers that question." I looked at Molly. "You didn't get any powers, right, Mols?"

My bestie suddenly found her biscuit very interesting.

"Mols?"

"Look at that bird," she finally said.

Rog and I looked and she laughed. "Gets you every time."

"In our defense," I said, "The occasional bird does get into The Muddle."

She snickered.

I decided it was time to change the subject. "I love the changes to the store, Mols."

Her pretty features lit with pleasure. "I do too! Since I needed to spend money to repair the damages anyway, I figured I might as well update the place to match my brand while I was at it."

"Matching her brand" translated to more recycled brick on the walls and floor, an expanded snack and juice bar, and several iconic urban features such as half of an old red truck and an antique sports car set into an area made to look like a city street. There was also a jungle area filled to the brim with tall palms and oversized concrete planters filled with flowers. The new beach area featured an entire wall painted like the ocean, as well as an enormous sand box where Molly planned to have all her beach and sun-wear displayed.

"The features will allow me to hold more photo shoots in the store instead of traveling to expensive locations." She shrugged. "It will save me a ton of money in the long run."

I was happy she'd once again turned lemons into lemonade. Her customers, who were already rabid fans and long-time friends, would flock to the new store and spend twice as much time there just because it was their favorite place to be. However...and there was always a however with a job like mine...I still felt guilty for dragging them into the mess. "I love it."

She narrowed her gaze on me, reading my body language as she always did. "Stop that. I'm not blaming you for what happened."

"But it was my fault you were taken."

She shook her head forcefully. "No, it wasn't. It was the

fault of a crazy sea horse who thought the world was hers to play with."

Rog glared at me. "Well, I do blame you. Molly and I were nearly killed by those beasts. As it is, I'm still having nightmares about them."

Molly rolled her eyes and I pressed my lips tight so I wouldn't smile. I happened to know that Rog had the time of his life on his adventure, with the not-so-minor exception of the Nessile bite, the healing of which he mostly slept through. Also, as he loved to remind us, he came out of the experience with temporary but exciting magical powers from his healing. "You told Molly you had fun."

He looked at Molly and frowned. "You told her that?"

Molly laughed. "Stop trying to make her feel bad. You loved having those kick-butt powers."

He tried to frown but failed. "It *was* kind of cool. Maybe Fair would be willing to visit once in a while and pump me full of magic again."

Okay, maybe he hadn't slept through *all* of his healing.

Molly and I shared a look. I gave up trying not to grin. "I think that one over there, with the rope swing, would be perfect."

Molly glanced toward the tree I was referencing. "Yep, that would work."

Rog frowned. "What are you two talking about?"

"You need a tree," Molly said, giving him a bright smile. For..."

We both sang, "Rog and Fair, sittin' in a tree, k-i-s-s-i-n-g."

As we laughed, he crossed skinny arms over his skinny chest. "Are you guys five years old?"

We laughed again.

I popped the last bite of biscuit into my mouth and ran a

hand over the smooth, uncracked top of the desk. "This no longer looks like an alien pod," I told my best friend. "How'd you fix it?"

She gave me a look. "You know I'm an engineering genius."

"Unhn." Molly could build the bejeezinx out of clothing, but she was even worse than Rog in assembling anything else. "Still. We kind of botched it irretrievably."

"You certainly did," she agreed unhappily. "It didn't help that you took one of the pieces with you into the rat ship."

I'd filled them in on what had happened as best I could. I figured I owed them that after what they'd gone through. They didn't like that Molly had been a pawn in the Nessile's crazy plans to force me into servitude, but it helped to understand why Molly had been taken and then basically just passed off to the strange, hermit-like sect of mole people. The Nessile had wanted to keep Molly out of sight for a while so she could keep using her as leverage against me. I had no doubt Elizabeth, my daughter, would have been next on the menu if the sea monster had needed more leverage against me.

"It's a good thing I took it," I told her. "It probably saved my life since I had no other weapons."

She frowned. "You need to practice more. Justice is right, you're not going to be safe until you have a better handle on your magic."

I bit my tongue, wanting to throttle my partner for engaging Molly to help threaten and shame me into training harder. I wondered what she'd think if she learned that I might have other magics, like the fish magic that had unexpectedly given me gills. There were likely other magics I didn't even know about yet that I'd need to train on too. "You don't need to pile on," I told her sourly. "I'm setting aside an hour every weekday and three hours on weekends to train."

She nodded. "Okay, I have something I need to do."

"Hold on," Rog said, raising a hand. "I want the truth. How did you get this desk together? I know you couldn't have salvaged the mess we left. Not by yourself."

Molly gave us a wink and a secretive grin. "Maybe I did have help."

Rog and I opened our mouths to argue with her. But we were distracted by a section of swirling air across the room.

My hand was on Rog's dropped butter knife in the time it took me to rise to my feet.

In a blink, Juggler appeared and lifted a hand. "Hello, Fishcakes." He frowned at the butter knife. "Am I in danger of being buttered to death?

I growled just a little bit. "Maybe. What are you doing here?"

He grinned, winking.

"You two can go home," Molly said, striding toward Juggler with an extra sway in her hips. "I'll see you on Monday."

Rog and I watched Juggler drop an arm around her waist and touch his lips tenderly to her temple. The annoying assistant and I shared a look. Then, as one, we started forward. "Oh, no you don't!" I yelled after the retreating pair.

"Overtime!" Rog yelled over me. "I have lots of paperwork to do, Mols. And I'm going to need your help."

They kept walking.

"Wait," I yelled. "You promised you'd help me plan the attack on the mole people and our rescue of the victims they're draining."

"Tomorrow," Molly threw over her shoulder.

"But..." I yelled.

"Wait..." Rog exclaimed.

A happy snicker wafted back to us as Molly and Juggler waved goodbye, and then disappeared into thin air.

"Argh!" I screamed.

Rog put hands on hips and glared at me. "This is all your fault. What are you going to do about it?" he demanded.

My lips flapped for a beat as I tried to think. What could I do? Molly was a grown woman. Juggler was a... He was a flippin' disaster. I turned on my heel and marched toward the door.

"Wait," Rog said. "Where do you think you're going?"

I yanked the door open and turned. "I'm going to do the only thing I'm good at. I'm going to go buy some shoes."

The End

DON'T MISS OUT

READ MORE MIDLIFE MUDDLE ADVENTURES

Book 1: One Bounce Away From Crazy

I always knew my shoe obsession would be the death of me. But I never guessed that murder would be involved.

My name is Raelynn Kitt. My friends call me Rae. My ex calls me Kitten, which is only one of the many reasons he's my ex. But that's not important. I have a confession to make.

I'm Rae, and I'm a shoe-aholic.

There are no church basement support groups for my addiction. No first-year chips to mark my progress in kicking the habit. Which wouldn't matter anyway since I haven't conquered it.

Not even close.

In fact, I blame my addiction for the recent chaotic turn of events in my life. Yeah, Karma is a jerk, and she just took a chunk out of my backside.

All because I couldn't walk past that cute little shoe store on the corner of Main and Fetter.

That was where a woman popped out of nowhere and died at my feet. Where the last words out of her mouth were to call me a Traveler. Hm. Then there's Justice. Not a legal concept, but a man who makes my heart stop for good and bad reasons. He thinks I'm a Traveler too. We're not talking about the packing a suitcase to go to the beach type of traveling.

Oh no. His kind of traveling involves monsters and visions.

I don't like his kind of traveling. But it's starting to look like I don't have a choice in the matter.

Am I a Traveler? Dancing goddess in yoga pants, I hope not.

Dang that cute little shoe store.

ONE BOUNCE AWAY FROM CRAZY

Shift Storm

"I'll take them both." Even as I said the words, I could feel panic flaring in my chest. Two more pairs of shoes. Two more expensive pairs. I was so out of control. If I kept up my current buying cycle, I'd have to remove furniture in my small apartment to make room for my shoes.

Maybe I could array them along the windowsills, like odd knickknacks. But then I'd have to dust them.

The thought set my knees a'knockin.

"That will be two-hundred-forty-two dollars and twenty-five cents."

I choked, quickly covering my lips with a fist and coughing delicately.

"Do you need a cup of water?" the petite, purple-haired twenty-something asked snidely.

"A..." I cleared my throat. "Allergies." I handed over my much-abused credit card, hoping its little silver tongue wasn't out and panting.

Despite my concern over spending the money, I held my

breath until the sale cleared, suddenly sure I'd drop dead if I didn't get the cute little pearl wedgies and the adorable sneakers with frayed edges.

The purple-haired young woman grabbed my receipt, smiling up at me. "Receipt in the bag or with you?"

"In the bag is fine," I answered by rote. I'd been through the process far too many times, it seemed.

She handed me my bag. "Thanks for coming in tonight."

I took it without comment, heading quickly toward the door. The deal done and my shame complete, I wanted to escape before anyone spotted me with my drug of choice.

The door jingled happily as I opened it. I ducked outside feeling like the little bell was laughing at me. Just another addict, shuffling away in shame.

Cool night air slipped over me, soft and fragrant with late spring flowers. I stood on the sidewalk and inhaled deeply, pulling the sweetness into my lungs.

Shame slipped away, pushed out by a potent combination of justifying thoughts and self-promises that I wouldn't buy any more shoes. Not for at least a year. Or six months. But then I realized I'd need new sandals when the cloying heat of an Indiana summer finally settled over the city.

Sighing, I turned my steps toward my apartment five blocks away, and determined to enjoy the rest of my walk.

Alas, it was not to be.

One minute, the sidewalk ahead of me was clear, the next, a woman was tumbling to the ground mere inches from my feet.

I jolted to a stop, but I wasn't fast enough. My black and white sneakers with the cute stacked heels smacked into her legs, sending me sprawling with a yelp. I landed in an ungainly pile, half over the woman and half draped along the sidewalk. My elbow barked at me where I'd scraped it along the concrete and the knee I'd hurt doing HIIT against my best friend's advice screamed with indignation.

Worse yet, The bag of shoes had smacked the poor woman right in the head. "Oh my gosh! I'm so sorry." I untangled myself from her and stood, grabbing at my bag. The twisted paper handle caught on her right ear and I yelped again, mortification clogging my lungs and making it hard to breathe. "Sorry! I'm so sorry. Are you okay?"

The woman didn't move. She lay there with her eyes closed, her flat chest barely rising and falling. Blood puddled beneath her head. Not a good sign. Had I done that with my shoe bag? "I'll call an ambulance," I promised her, though there was little indication she could hear me. I dug in my purse for my phone, not finding it for a full minute. Just when my hand felt the familiar smooth rectangle, something clamped around my ankle.

"Ah!" I tried to yank away but the woman's hand was like a vise on my leg. Seeing her pale, amber eyes fixed on me, I felt relief. "You're going to be all right," I told her, pulling the phone out of my purse, "I'm calling for an ambulance." I punched 9-1-1.

The woman's eyes closed briefly, then reopened. Her grip on my ankle tightened painfully.

I winced. "You can let go of me now," I said, my voice only slightly strained. "You've got my attention."

But she didn't let go. In fact, her grip tightened more. Then her lips moved. I couldn't hear what she was saying, so I crouched down, dropping to my knees as she finally released me. "What did you say?" I lowered my ear to within a couple of inches of her face. "Say it again."

The hand that had gripped my ankle found my arm. Cool fingers wrapped around my wrist and the woman's amber eyes found mine. "Trav..." She stopped, her chest heaving.

"I'm listening," I urged her.

She swallowed hard. "Traveler Kitt." Light flared into the night, as blinding as headlights but brighter. The light hurt my eyes and I squinted, trying to avert my gaze. But I realized the illumination wasn't coming from the street. It was coming from the woman. Her hand on my wrist felt burning hot, like flame against my skin. I tried to yank away from her but she held on, burning my arm where she touched. A blink later, her body convulsed, arching off the sidewalk so that only her head and heels still touched the ground. Then, in the blink of an eye, the light was gone.

And so was the woman.

***

Emergency lights throbbed a steady beat. The ambulance was stopped at an odd angle from the curb, two cop cars making it impossible for them to park any other way. The lights on all three vehicles pulsed against the darkness, painting all of us standing on the sidewalk in a strange watercolor flush.

"I swear, the woman was right there." I frowned at the spot on the sidewalk where the pool of blood had been. "And she was bleeding from a head wound. I thought I'd hurt her with my bag when I tripped over her..." I trailed off, seeing the disbelieving gazes of the two young cops who I thankfully didn't know as I told my impossible story. "She was there," I insisted.

"Then where'd she go?" the male cop asked. His face looked so young I doubted he even needed to shave. His uniform seemed too big on him. The woman was two inches taller than the male cop. She filled out her uniform in a way that most men would probably find appealing. But her eyes were hard and she hadn't stopped glaring at me since they'd arrived on the scene.

I was used to that reaction from female cops. They'd heard the stories. Whether I liked it or not, I was something of a legend at the FWPD.

"Detective Kitt, have you been drinking?"

"I'm no longer a detective. I'm retired." Both her accusation and her manner were insulting. "I haven't been drinking, Officer..." I squinted at her badge, letting her know I didn't recognize her. "Does that say Sparkle?" I grinned and she stiffened.

"Spargle," the cop ground out with irritation.

"Officer *Spargle*. I don't drink. I don't do drugs. I fell over the woman." Inspiration flared and I lifted my arm to show them my skinned elbow. "See?"

"That certainly seems to suggest you fell down," the male cop said. His mid-range voice was thick with mockery.

I stared at them for a long moment, frustrated and unsure what to do. Somewhere there was a badly injured woman, and I had no idea how to help her. The problem was, I'd been in those cops' shoes. I understood their position. I looked like a crazy lady. Heck, if I hadn't seen it with my own eyes, I'd think I was crazy too. But I *had* seen it. I opened my mouth again and Officer Sparkle-Spargle turned away, waving toward the EMTs. "There's nothing here. You can go."

I gritted my teeth as the EMTs threw me a pitying look and climbed back into the ambulance.

"If there's nothing else Mrs. Kitt," the woman cop said.

I might have growled a little. There was only one thing I hated more than my currently embarrassing situation and that was being called Mrs. Kitt. I was no longer a Mrs. and

Kitt was my maiden name, not my married name. "I guess not, Officer Sparkle."

The woman glared at me, but inclined her head and turned away. The male cop said, "Good night," avoiding my name altogether, and followed her to the street. I didn't wait around to watch them leave. I took off down the street without looking back.

If ever there was a time I wished I could drink...

Get your copy here: https://books2read.com/bounce

ABOUT THE AUTHOR

USA Today and Wall Street Journal Bestselling Author Sam Cheever writes mystery and suspense, creating stories that draw you in and keep you eagerly turning pages. Known for writing great characters, snappy dialogue, and unique and exhilarating stories, Sam is the award-winning author of 100+ books.

To learn more about Sam and her work, visit her at one of her online hotspots:
www.samcheever.com
samcheever@samcheever.com

ALSO BY SAM CHEEVER

If you enjoyed **A Bounce Before I Die**, you might also enjoy these other fun series by Sam. To find out more, visit the **BOOKS** page at www.samcheever.com:

Midlife Muddle Paranormal Women's Fiction - For more fun with Rae and the gang!

Mature Magic Paranormal Women's Fiction

Enchanting Inquiries Paranormal Cozy Mysteries

Yesterday's Paranormal Mysteries

Reluctant Familiar Paranormal Mysteries

Grave Theatrics Mysteries

Country Cousin Mysteries

Silver Hills Cozy Mysteries

Gainfully Employed Mysteries

Honeybun Heat Series